Inspector Forsooth's
Whodunits

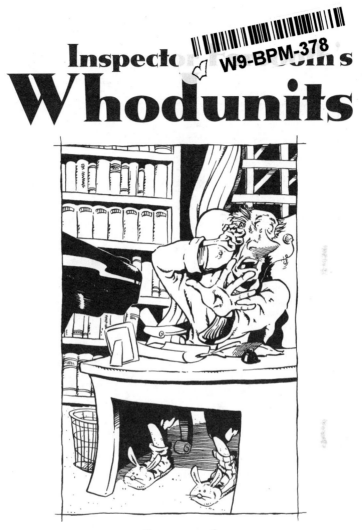

Derrick Niederman

Illustrated by Matt LaFleur

Sterling Publishing Co., Inc.
New York

Thanks go to my many friends at America Online—Mary Ann Schwartz, Terry Morse, Lyn Cameron, Amy Arnold, Beth Gonzales, Robert J. Scott, Mirenda Howard, and Heather Matys. I'm also indebted to Chris Dwyer, Rob Blaustein, and James Niederman for fielding my technical inquiries, and to Lee Meriwether for assisting me with "The Valentine's Day Massacre." And of course I owe a great debt to the hundreds of online sleuths who participated in "The Sunday Night Mystery," with a special thanks to Iampeg, the most devoted sleuth of them all.

Library of Congress Cataloging-in-Publication Data

Niederman, Derrick.
    Inspector Forsooth's whodunits / Derrick Niederman ; illustrated by Matt LaFleur.
      p. cm.
    Summary: Twelve stories each with a question and answer section at the end to help solve the mysteries. Provides answers at the back of the book.
    ISBN 0-8069-3182-5
    1. Detective and mystery stories. [1. Mystery and detective stories. 2. Short stories.] I. LaFleur, Matt, ill. II. Title.
PZ7.N5635In 1998
[Fic]-dc21

          98-39763
          CIP
          AC

10 9 8 7 6 5 4 3 2 1

First paperback edition published in 1999 by
Sterling Publishing Company, Inc.
387 Park Avenue South, New York, N.Y. 10016
© 1998 by Derrick Niederman
Some of these stories are reprinted from the Murder Mystery Forum with the permission of America Online. AOL and America Online are registered trademarks of America Online, in the United States and other countries.
Distributed in Canada by Sterling Publishing
% Canadian Manda Group, One Atlantic Avenue, Suite 105
Toronto, Ontario, Canada M6K 3E7
Distributed in Great Britain and Europe by Cassell PLC
Wellington House, 125 Strand, London WC2R 0BB, England
Distributed in Australia by Capricorn Link (Australia) Pty Ltd.
P.O. Box 6651, Baulkham Hills, Business Centre, NSW 2153, Australia
Manufactured in the United States of America
All rights reserved

Sterling ISBN 0-8069-3182-5 Trade
          0-8069-3199-X Paper

Contents

INTRODUCTION

THE MYSTERIES IN THIS BOOK are like no others you've ever tried. For starters, they've all been tested live—in an America Online "auditorium"—in front of hundreds of cybersleuths. These intrepid sleuths would read the mystery text and then fire literally thousands of questions at yours truly, Inspector Forsooth. The questions and answers that accompany each mystery are taken directly from these online solving sessions.

Sound interesting? Good. It gets even better.

These mysteries go far beyond the "one-shot wonder" format that dominates the mini-mystery genre. (You've seen such stories, I'm sure. Like the English professor who "committed suicide" and left a note filled with grammatical errors.) Such mysteries can be entertaining—I've tried hundreds of them myself. But aren't you ready for something a bit more challenging? Something new and different? You've come to the right place.

Each of the mysteries in this book contains a mosaic of clues that the sleuth (that's you) must piece together to divine the solution. You will be aided by the question-and-answer session—an edited version of the real-time, online chaos—which flushes out each and every tiny clue hidden in the text. You can read all the answers or test yourself by reading only a few. It's all up to you.

I feel I should warn you, though: These mysteries are hard! They're not child's play. But I'm confident you'll love the challenges I have for you.

Inspector Forsooth
Cybersleuth Extraordinaire

MURDER AROUND THE CLOCK

BRUCE BERRINGER WAS A SUCCESSFUL MAN, but he paid a high price. When all was said and done, his success cost him his life.

Berringer was born and raised in the small town of Bogusville, near the Colorado/Utah border. His was a blue-collar community, and the townsfolk were the sort of friendly, hardworking, generous souls that so often come out of rural America. But Berringer wanted more. He wanted money, prestige, and a name for himself in international business circles.

He had the smarts, the drive, and the connections to make good on his dream. His father was a Navy man who had traveled all over the world prior to returning to Bogusville, and Bruce's business savvy parlayed these far-flung contacts into a thriving importing enterprise: pottery, belts, wicker—you name it. Berringer Imports grew to the point where it had satellite offices literally around the world. But rather than leave his roots, Berringer delighted in keeping his main office right at home, knowing he could parade his success in front of all those who thought he'd never amount to anything in this world.

As a result of Berringer's obsession with fame, friendships suffered. His childhood cronies noticed that Berringer judged them by what they did for a living and not who they were as people. None of them made one-tenth the money Berringer did, and his scorn was always there.

One night there was a big party at Berringer Imports to celebrate the landing of a new international account. Five of Bruce's friends from high school showed up. They didn't necessarily want to be there, and they certainly didn't fit in with the corporate types who flew in for the occasion; but in some sense it was worse to be left out of the lavish Berringer celebrations than to suffer through one night. Liked or not, Berringer was the most powerful figure in town, and he could be very vengeful when people didn't play the games he wanted them to.

The cronies included Rafael Betz, who owned a catering business and was doing well in his own right, in no small part because he had the opportunity to cater many of Berringer's parties, including this particular one. Then there was Frank Dowling, a plumbing contractor, who complained that the ultra-rich Berringer was incredibly cheap, haggling over charges that normal people would pay without comment. The other local guests were rated even lower on Berringer's importance scale. There was Sean McGillicuddy, whose DairyFresh route took him to the outskirts of the Berringer estate but never any farther, and there was Jimmie Wu, who scratched out a living by refereeing local high school athletic contests, including many involving Berringer's spoiled son Yancey. About the only one of Berringer's buddies who looked comfortable at this black-tie affair was Benjamin Walters, but only because he was accustomed to formalities. Walters was the maître d' at the swank Olivia's restaurant, which was started with money from—you guessed it—Bruce Berringer. Berringer even got a rare laugh by raising his arm and calling out "Maître d'!" upon spying Walters at the party in his usual tuxedo.

Most of the guests had a decent enough time that night. The oyster bar was fully stocked, and the champagne was flowing. But trouble lurked. After the party, Berringer went back to his desk at the other side of the office complex to tidy up some unfinished business, never mind how late it was. He was discovered the next morning, sitting at his desk, with two gunshot wounds in his chest. He was as dead as a smelt. The time of his death was later estimated to be between 12:00 midnight and 2:00 a.m., Mountain Time.

The most curious aspect of the crime scene was a note that Berringer had left on the pink notepad on his desk. The note said simply: "1:30 hence...," then it trailed off. The note had presumably been written after the shots were fired, in the limited amount of time that he had remaining.

Because Berringer's five school buddies were the last people to leave the party, they were considered the primary suspects. It turned out that four of them had gone out after the party, and each could vouch for the others' whereabouts. When told about Berringer's note, they confirmed that they were still together at 1:30. The only exception was Jimmie Wu, who didn't like the idea of all-night carousing, given that he was supposed to be a stern, proper official for the community. Wu insisted that he had gone straight to bed, but he had no one who could corroborate his story.

When Inspector Forsooth visited the crime scene, he looked up at the wall outside Berringer's office. There, through the glass, he saw a row of clocks, each displaying the time at one of Berringer Imports' offices around the world. First there was a clock labeled "Chicago," which was Berringer's first office outside of Bogusville. The row continued with the other six office sites, in order of their establishment: Paris, Los Angeles, Cairo, Mexico City, Caracas, and New York. Berringer liked to be able to look up from his office and see immediately what the time was throughout his empire. That way he could keep even better tabs on all his regional managers, all of whom he lorded over like a drill sergeant.

Forsooth studied the clocks as if in a trance, until one of the other detectives interrupted him. "Inspector, you okay?" Forsooth nodded. The detective then asked, "Any idea how we're going to locate the killer?" There was a short pause, and then Forsooth issued a curiously short reply: "Time will tell."

1) Who killed Bruce Berringer?

2) How can the other suspects be ruled out?

INSPECTOR FORSOOTH ANSWERS YOUR QUESTIONS

Q1–Were the clocks digital or analog?

They were analog. Had the clocks been digital, the killer might still be loose! (Remember, all the questions are actual questions from online sleuths. They didn't have the benefit of the illustration at the beginning of this story!)

Q2–If the high school cronies hated Berringer, why were they at the party?

Because Berringer was a vindictive, petty man, and there was no telling what he might do if they didn't show up to admire his wealth. Better to grin and bear it through one night.

Q3–Did it matter that Berringer's father was in the Navy?

Yes. It meant that Berringer was familiar with the concept of a distress signal, which is precisely what he was trying to convey in his note.

Q4–Was the murder committed at 1:30?

No, it was not.

Q5–Is the order of the clocks important?

Absolutely. Theoretically, though, you could deduce the answer without knowing the order!

Q6–Is the number of clocks important?

Even more important than the order, in some sense. The fact that there were seven clocks is central to the solution.

Q7–Were the clocks arranged in some sort of code?

They sure were. Semaphore code, to be precise, which Berringer probably picked up from his father.

Q8–Do you need to know semaphore code to be able to solve the mystery?

No, you do not—would I do that to you? All you need to

know is that semaphore code is given using flags and different positions of the arms—much like the hands of a clock. Each letter of the alphabet can be depicted by a specific position of the flags—or hands, as the case may be.

Q9–Dowling and Walters are the only two suspects whose names have seven letters. Does that mean one of them killed Bruce Berringer?

Believe it or not, the length of their names is not important.

Q10–Is the location of the offices important?

In general, no. But the location of a couple of them can lead you to the murderer.

Q11–When did the murder actually take place?

The murder took place at just after midnight. The "hence" in Berringer's note meant "in the future," not "therefore." You could use semaphore code to determine the precise time!

Q12–Is it significant that Berringer addressed Walters as "Maître d' "?

Yes, it's extremely significant. Remember, Berringer cared more about what people did than who they were. But in order to identify the killer, you're still going to have to supply one teensy-weensy ingredient that hasn't been covered in these 12 questions.

Can you solve the mystery?

Solution on page 80.

WARM-BLOODED MURDER

WHEN THE VOTES HAD BEEN COUNTED in the New Hampshire Republican primary of 1996, you could see the usual assortment of reactions: Pat Buchanan was rejoicing in victory, Bob Dole was putting the best spin on the slender margin of his defeat, and so on, from Steve Forbes and Lamar Alexander all the way down to the unheralded Michael Doucette.

But for the residents of Jasper Falls, New Hampshire, the day's political events were overshadowed by the stunning announcement that local political operative Vince Fernald, a mainstream Republican, had been bludgeoned to death. Jasper Falls was located not far from Dixville Notch, which had become famous for its position as the first town in the nation to get up and vote on election day. So politics were a pretty serious business in that neck of the woods, and getting more serious all the time.

Fernald's body had been found in a trash dumpster behind the town hall. The town hall served as the polling place for the community, and the small patch of land in back happened to abut Fernald's own backyard. His body was discovered late in the afternoon by a man named Clem Woolsey, a state employee who ran the garbage collection service for all the towns in the area. Tuesday was his regular day to service Jasper Falls, but in this case he had come to vote. In deference to the nature of his job, Woolsey had gone home and cleaned up after work that day, but once he got to the town hall he couldn't resist sneaking a peek in back to see how much trash was accumulating. To his horror, he noticed a foot sticking out of the dumpster, and when he summoned help to probe further, Fernald's scantily clad corpse was uncovered. Fernald's head had been struck several times, and a pool of blood had collected on one of the trash bags beneath his body.

In the wake of this grisly discovery, some curious facts emerged. One was that Fernald's overcoat was found in a park several miles from the murder site. The other curiosity was that candidate Michael Doucette, although winning less than one percent of the statewide vote, had received almost twenty percent of the vote in Jasper Falls! Something very fishy was going on.

Suspicion immediately fell on local Doucette supporters Hugh Livingston and Clancy McTigue, but both men appeared to have ironclad alibis. Livingston had been campaigning in Manchester and Concord during the weekend, and had driven back up Tuesday morning to place his vote at one of the two temporary booths set up at the Jasper Falls town hall. He remained at the voting area holding a Doucette sign throughout the day, the only exception being when he went out by himself for a late lunch at Charlie's Diner. Livingston was known in town for his ardent conservative stances, and his man Doucette made Pat Buchanan look like Jerry Brown. But as fearsome as Livingston was politically, it wasn't at all clear that a killer lurked inside.

As for McTigue, he had been in Jasper Falls trying to drum up local support for Doucette in the days before the primary. McTigue noted that he had been at the town hall practically all of election day. When asked about lunch, he said that he, too, had gone to Charlie's Diner: Unlike Livingston, however, he had eaten with several other Doucette supporters, any one of whom could attest to his whereabouts. After lunch, he went directly to the town hall to place his vote, and remained there afterwards.

Suspicion was also cast on a stranger in town, a reporter named Luc Evans-Wood, who lived well away from Jasper Falls. Evans-Wood said he had driven down the previous night in order to cover the primaries for his town newspaper. He also said the assignment had come at the last minute, so he had to sleep in his car. When asked whether it wasn't too cold to stay outside, he replied that he was a hardy soul, and he had been warned beforehand that the temperatures weren't apt to exceed five degrees. In his car was found an article praising Michael Doucette, but Evans-Wood said the article had been mailed to him, and it just happened to have arrived the day before. He admitted to being politically conservative, but denied any interest in Doucette or any personal stake in the outcome of the election.

Finally, Clem Woolsey, the man who had discovered Fernald's body in the first place, was told that he had been seen earlier that day driving his trash truck near the area where the dead man's coat had been found. Woolsey didn't seem surprised, and claimed that his appearance there was consistent with his trash pickup schedule, although he acknowledged that it was two towns over from Jasper Falls. Woolsey also claimed that he had voted for Bob Dole, and was just as frustrated as other Dole supporters concerning their candidate's unusually poor showing in Jasper Falls. The Dole group protested that the election had been rigged, but there was never any evidence to support that claim.

When the authorities had the chance to review the case, they concluded that the most likely reason Vince Fernald had been killed was that he had simply been in the wrong place at the wrong time. But you must go a step further. Here are the questions you must answer:

1) Who killed Vince Fernald and why?

2) What are the alibis for the other suspects?

3) How did an examination of the voting records help the investigation?

INSPECTOR FORSOOTH ANSWERS YOUR QUESTIONS

Q1–Did Jasper Falls have a regular trash pickup that day, considering that it was an election day?

Good question, and I hope I don't mislead you with my response. The answer is that on a primary day, work goes on as usual. It's up to employers to understand that people need to vote.

Q2–Is the timing of the primary important?

It sure is. It's pretty much impossible to make all the details fit without knowing when (calendar-wise) the crime occurred.

Q3–Did Fernald discover that votes were being tampered with?

It certainly looks as though he came across some high jinks at the town hall. It's a reasonable assumption that this discovery led to his murder.

Q4–Had Clem already serviced Jasper Falls prior to going to vote?

I love this question. It's another one that I hope I answer properly, without any misleading. But the answer is no.

Q5–Within the voting booth, are the candidates listed in alphabetical order?

Yes, they are.

Q6–The text refers to a "pool of blood" in the dumpster. Does this mean that it wasn't frozen? Is this an important detail?

The blood was most definitely not frozen. Is this an important detail? Well, it does seem to relate to the issue of how long the body had been in the dumpster. Let's just say that you're going to have to account for this issue in your solution!

Q7–But the mystery indicates that Clem had finished his

work that day. How do you explain the fact that he hadn't gotten to the town hall dumpster?

One possibility is that the body was dumped off after Clem finished his rounds. But there is another, even better possibility that you should be thinking of.

Q8–Did Luc Evans-Wood cast a vote that day?

No. I can say with complete certainty that Luc did not cast a vote that day, either in Jasper Falls or anywhere else.

Q9–What date was the murder?

Tuesday, February 20, 1996. That was the date of the 1996 New Hampshire primary.

Q10–If it was only five degrees out, how was Evans-Wood able to spent the night in his car?

Well, remember that he is the one who gave us the temperature in the first place. A very important fact!

Q11–Was the work week delayed because of Presidents' Day?

Bingo. That's why the timing of the murder is so important. In fact, now we know a little bit more about the timing!

Q12–If the murder occurred the day after Presidents' Day, how could Evans-Wood have received a letter the day before? Isn't he lying?

Not necessarily. Note that he had driven "down" to cover the primaries. When you consider that Dixville Notch—and therefore Jasper Falls—are in northernmost New Hampshire, you should see what I'm driving at.

Can you solve the mystery?

Solution on page 91.

HALLOWEEN HORROR

BEING A GHOST FOR HALLOWEEN IS one thing. Becoming a ghost is another. But that's what happened to one teenage girl on this scariest of Halloweens.

The trick-or-treating part of the evening went about as expected, with house after house trembling as her wispy figure made its way up the front steps. The ghost lived in a town where folks took their costumes seriously, and people were especially generous to inspired creations. By the time the night was through, she had amassed enough goodies to last her until Thanksgiving. But she didn't last even one day, thanks to a fatal choice of late-night snack.

In the ghost's possession at the time of her death was a half-eaten Butterfinger bar, which was immediately sent to the toxicology lab. The results showed that the candy bar had been laced with rat poison: It must have been doctored and rewrapped, but the ghost never noticed it. But even if the question of how she died could be resolved, it wasn't at all clear who might have wanted her out of the way.

In real life, the ghost was in junior high school. She was a good student, seemingly without an enemy in the world. She was also a shoo-in to make the cheerleading squad for the upcoming basketball season. And with that small fact, a motive began to take shape. The problem was that the candy bar could have come from virtually anybody along her Halloween route.

The ghost's route on her final Halloween journey was painstakingly retraced, and some curious facts turned up: For one, she had been trick-or-treating with a group of friends until fairly late in the evening, and all were pretty sure that the ghost hadn't picked up any Butterfinger bars during their escapades. But after leaving her friends, she had gone to four houses in a final circle near her own home. And of those four families, three of them had a daughter who was vying for the same cheerleading squad! The families in question were the Ackmans, the Bartosavages, and the Claxtons, whom the

19

ghost visited in that order. Her final stop came at Old Lady MacDonald's house up on the hill; the old lady was a widow, and her kids had all grown up and moved away.

The interviews with these residents left the police no closer than they had been at first. Everyone professed outrage at the heinous Halloween crime that had shaken the neighborhood. Each said that the ghost was one of the last trick-or-treaters they had that night (the earlier part of the evening having been taken up with younger kids), and each of them fiercely denied an attempt to poison for the sake of cheerleading—although they had all heard stories about such overzealous parents.

Not wanting to miss any detail, the police compiled records of how everyone was disguised that night. It turned out that Mr. Ackman had greeted his arrivals in his customary devil suit. Mrs. Bartosavage had greeted her callers in a light-up skeleton costume whose bones glowed in the dark. Mr. Claxton had devised a special outfit in which a woman's mask, etc., were placed on his back, so that he approached his guests facing backwards! When he turned around, the effect was creepy indeed. And Old Lady MacDonald, who was approaching 80 years of age, rose to the occasion by simply taking out her dentures and painting her face green. That, coupled with a mole or two on her cheek, made her the scariest witch of the night.

Of these four houses, only two—the Ackmans and the Bartosavages—had any Butterfinger bars remaining from Halloween. The ones they had left over were tested for rat poison, but those tests all came back negative. As for the Claxtons, they claimed to have treated visitors with many other items—M&Ms, Hershey's, and Mars bars, among others. As for Mrs. MacDonald, she was known to be the least generous of all the neighborhood stops, and she only had licorice and saltwater taffy, which some trick-or-treaters suspected had been left over from the previous year!

One question that puzzled the investigators was that there had been two other girls who paraded through the neighborhood just before the ghost came. The first had been dressed as Mary Poppins. The second—wouldn't you know it—came dressed as a cheerleader. And both of them were trying out for the cheerleading team in real life. The existence of these two girls threw a monkey wrench into the entire investigation, because it wasn't clear whether the ghost had been singled out, or whether the killer would have been happy to knock anyone off just to create one more space on the squad.

However, Inspector Forsooth thought it extremely likely that the ghost had in fact been singled out of the crowd. Acting on that assumption, he was able to identify the perpetrator.

1) Who killed the ghost?

2) How could the killer feel confident that no one other than the intended victim would be killed by the poison?

3) How did the killer's choice of costume play a role?

INSPECTOR FORSOOTH ANSWERS YOUR QUESTIONS

Q1–Was the victim still wearing her costume when she died?
No, she was not wearing her costume.

Q2–How did the killer know who the ghost was?
The killer found out through the grapevine, meaning that there was discussion about who was dressing up as what, so the ghost's identity was known in advance.

Q3–Was there anyone else dressed as a ghost that night?
Not in that neighborhood, no.

Q4–How did they know she would pick that particular Butterfinger bar?
It was the only Butterfinger bar there!

Q5–Did any of the people in the suspect houses know that the victim was coming by?

No. They had no idea who was coming until they got there.

Q6–Does the fact that the ghost left her friends to go alone have any significance?

Yes, it is quite significant. Had the ghost not gone out alone, there could never have been any assurance that she would pick up the tainted bar.

Q7–Was it important that the ghost was one of the last trick-or-treaters?

It sure was.

Q8–Did the ghost choose her own candy, or was it handed to her?

Great question. The ghost chose her own candy.

Q9–Were Butterfingers the victim's favorite candy bar?

No, they weren't necessarily her favorite, but they were certainly preferable to other choices.

Q10–So the widow, who had bad candy, wanted the cheerleader dead, and she put a good candy in the bad candy?

I didn't say that! What motive could she possibly have had?

Q11–What do Mrs. MacDonald's teeth have to do with it?

Well, remember that the killer wasn't taking any chances that the poisoned Butterfinger bar might end up in the wrong hands—or mouth.

Q12–Did the Mary Poppins carry an umbrella?

Sure did. And you're on the right track—but it looks as though you have to dig a little deeper.

Can you solve the mystery?

Solution on page 79.

THE PRINTS OF LIGHTNESS

AFTER IT WAS ALL OVER, the workmen outside Oscar Delahanty's home could barely comprehend the irony of what had
just taken place. The men had arrived promptly at 8:30 one
summer morning to install a roadside fire hydrant some fifty
feet or so from Delahanty's front walkway. Barely an hour into
their job, well before the new hydrant was operational, they
saw smoke billowing out of a first-floor window. They con-
tacted their buddies at the fire department, who got down as
quickly as they could. However, by the time the firefighters
arrived, Delahanty's small but historic home had already sus-
tained significant damage. And that wasn't all.

When the firemen on the scene trudged upstairs to Delahanty's bedroom, they found him lying in bed, quite dead. He was
still dressed in his blue silk pajamas, so clearly he hadn't enjoyed
much of this sultry summer morning. The fire itself hadn't
reached the upstairs, but there was plenty of smoke all around.
The firemen couldn't help but notice that the window in his
bedroom, which looked out onto the road, was firmly shut.

The blaze had apparently started near the back door, which
was part of the "newer" section of the house. By the looks of
things, the hardwood floors in that area, including the back
staircase, had just been refinished, but they had been almost
completely torched by the blaze. Officials couldn't be certain
just what had been used to ignite the fire, but they doubted
that it had started by accident.

The fire chief noted that everything in the house seemed to
be in compliance with local regulations. However, he couldn't
help but note that older houses were notoriously poor fire
risks, and an alarm system that was directly wired into the fire
department would have saved time and prevented some of the
damage they were witnessing. Implicit in his remark was that
a better system might have saved Delahanty's life.

The next step was to alert Delahanty's employees at The
Clip Joint, the hair salon he had owned and operated for just
over six years. When the authorities got there, they could see

that it was a busy morning, rendered all the busier by the boss's no-show. The three stylists on the job were Ginger LaCroix, Stan Norton, and Mitchell Quinn, each of whom had worked for Delahanty since the salon opened. When told that their boss had died of asphyxia, all three were momentarily speechless. After this stunned silence was over, Quinn said he would phone the boss's other appointments and officially cancel them. Ginger LaCroix had already placed a call to Delahanty's home, but had gotten only his answering machine. She asked if the house was damaged in the fire, and expressed relief that it could probably be rebuilt. As for Stan Norton, he had apparently been planning on visiting the boss's home himself to see what was wrong, but now he did not have to.

The investigators took careful note of these various reactions, but it wasn't until 24 hours had elapsed that a possible motive appeared. A woman named Hilda Graylock came forward to say that Delahanty had offered her a job as a stylist with his salon. He indicated to her that he was planning on letting one of his staff go, but she didn't know which one. To make matters even more interesting, not long after Graylock gave her testimony, another woman appeared at the police station and gave the exact same story! These tidbits certainly changed the complexion of things, and, upon consultation with the medical examiner, police now concluded definitively that Delahanty had been murdered.

Upon returning to the salon, the authorities picked up some more information about what happened that morning. Mitchell Quinn testified that he had opened up the salon at 8:00 a.m. It was The Clip Joint's policy to rotate the responsibility for the 8:00 shift; the rest of the staff would come in later in the morning, well in time for the lunchtime crunch. The salon stayed open until 8:30 at night, and the bulk of its business was conducted at lunchtime and during the evening hours.

As it happened, everyone had worked late the night before Delahanty's death. LaCroix and Norton had gone out for a drink and a bite to eat afterwards; they were joined by a couple from the massage studio located right next to The Clip Joint. That little gathering didn't break up until about midnight, whereupon everybody went home. As for the next morning, LaCroix had come in about 9:30, while Norton had arrived at a couple of minutes past ten, something of an annoyance to his 10:00 appointment.

A revisiting of the crime scene offered a couple of important details. Ordinarily, the back door to Delahanty's home would have been locked with a dead bolt, which was of course activated from the inside. But whoever had done the floorwork had exited that way, and was unable to lock the door on the way out! So that explained how the killer could have entered the home without forced entry and without the workmen seeing him or her. Because of the layout of the house, it would have been quite easy for someone to have entered the back way without being spotted.

Upon hearing this crucial piece of information, Hilda Graylock lamented Delahanty's bad luck. He had evidently sought permission from the town clerk's office for several months to get the floors redone. (Because much of the house dated back to the early 18th century, it had attained landmark status, so he couldn't do much without the town's approval.) However, the "newer" wing, although still a century old, did not have quite the same restrictions, so the work was approved, as long as the wood was stained in a manner consistent with the rest of the woodwork. And just a day after the work was complete, Delahanty was dead.

Before the authorities could get around to identifying the murderer, they received more than they could possibly have hoped for—a confession. That's right, one of Delahanty's employees admitted to having killed the boss. Ordinarily the investigation might have ended right then and there, but in this case police truly got too much of a good thing. Later that same day, another Clip Joint employee admitted to having killed Delahanty! Neither confession could be readily dismissed. In fact, both people took lie detector tests, and they each passed with flying colors.

The bad news was that some important evidence had been destroyed. The good news was that the coroner's report turned out to invalidate one of the two confessions. Even without seeing that report, do you know who the real murderer was? Well, it's not easy, and a couple of issues will have to be resolved in the question-and-answer session that follows. But here are the questions you must answer:

1) Who killed Oscar Delahanty?

2) Who wrongly confessed to the crime?

3) How did the coroner's report help identify the killer?

4) What was the "evidence" that was destroyed?

INSPECTOR FORSOOTH ANSWERS YOUR QUESTIONS

Q1–Could Ginger or Stan have killed him the prior night?

No. The folks at the massage studio could attest to their whereabouts all night.

Q2–Why is it important that Delahanty lived in a landmark house?

Because it wouldn't have been possible for him to have central air conditioning. (The fact that his bedroom window was closed suggests that there was no room air conditioner either.)

Q3–Since more than one person was being hired, does that mean that more than one person was being fired?

It certainly looks that way.

Q4–Did the floor refinishers leave the night before? If so, why didn't Delahanty check to make sure the doors were locked before going to bed?

The workmen had in fact left the night before, but they had essentially "painted in" the area near the back door, so Delahanty couldn't have gone in that area (i.e., to lock the door) without ruining the new finish.

Q5–Why was Ginger so concerned about the house?

Perhaps she had a sentimental streak, and didn't really like the idea of such a nice home being destroyed.

Q6–When the police said that the victim had been "asphyxiated," does that mean that he died of smoke inhalation?

Not necessarily. "Asphyxiation" technically refers to any situation where breathing is impaired, whether arising from smoke inhalation, strangulation, or whatever.

Q7–Did the house's landmark status mean that it couldn't have smoke alarms?

Not at all. In fact, it was even more important for Delahanty to have smoke alarms, precisely because antique houses are extremely flammable. And the fire chief would certainly have noticed had Delahanty's smoke alarms been absent or defective.

Q8–Why was a hydrant being installed at that particular location?

Pure chance. Presumably the town had simply decided that it needed more hydrants, and noted that there wasn't one close enough to Oscar and his neighbors. (On a personal note, Inspector Forsooth returned home one evening to find a fire hydrant installed on the road alongside his own house. It does happen!)

Q9–Did the work on the hydrant begin that day or earlier?

Great question. The answer is that the work began that very morning.

Q10–If it was a sultry morning, why were Oscar's windows closed?

Another excellent question. We can assume that Delahanty wouldn't have been able to get to sleep that night had his windows been closed.

Q11–Had the floor fully dried?

Given what we know about the weather, etc., it seems unlikely that the finish would have been perfectly dry. Some polyurethane finishes can take a full 24 hours to dry.

Q12–How many workmen does it take to install a fire hydrant?

No light bulb jokes, please. The answer is that it takes several people to do the job, primarily because they have to jack-hammer through the pavement to get to the pipes.

Can you solve the mystery?

Solution on page 86.

THE FINAL FORECLOSURE

IT WAS A SITUATION THAT HAD trouble written all over it. Niles Bronson was involved in the Ocean Towers condominium in every conceivable way: He had lived there since 1992, when the building was first constructed; he managed the condo fund, which covered all the routine expenses shared by the building's inhabitants; finally, he worked at Marine Bank, which held the mortgages on many of the condominium properties.

Several of Niles's colleagues on the condo board felt that he had conflicts of interest on the various matters that came before them. Others felt that he simply held too much influence, period. So when he was found dead in his living room one late-March evening in 1996, everyone figured it was an inside job.

No murder weapon was ever recovered, despite an immediate and exhaustive search of the entire condominium complex. But the suspicion of an "inside job" was only amplified when a search of the documents in Bronson's files revealed that three of the building's residents were facing foreclosure proceedings. That group consisted of Herman Gertner (like Bronson, a resident of Ocean Towers since its inception), real estate developer Graham Moss, and Jeff Carrington, who at one time had been a thriving restaurateur.

Each of the three men faced his own special type of financial distress. Carrington had been tracked down by his ex-wife and now faced substantial child support payments. Moss had leveraged himself to the hilt constructing an office building that was proving to be a dismal failure. And Gertner was withholding his mortgage payments until certain long-promised improvements were made to his property. Although the three men's predicaments were entirely different, what they had in common was that each had failed to meet his mortgage payments for several months. And that fact alone placed them under great scrutiny following the murder.

Actually, whoever killed Niles Bronson was lucky not to

have been unmasked right away. A Mrs. Rose Kravitz, who lived in Suite 1507, just around the corner from Bronson's Suite 1516, claimed that she had passed a strange man in the hallway as she took out the garbage late that afternoon. Ocean Towers was a fairly small, close-knit community; those on any particular floor tended to recognize those from the same floor, and this man simply didn't belong. At the time, though, Rose didn't think much about the stranger, nor did she get a good look at him. All she remembered was that he was wearing a T-shirt and some cut-off blue jeans.

That same evening, Rose had some business to discuss with Niles Bronson, and she was perplexed when he didn't answer her knock—hadn't he said he would be in? She said that she had made sure to knock at halftime of the NCAA semifinal game between UMass and Kentucky, in order not to catch him at a bad time. She could hear the TV from outside, though, and became suspicious when her repeated knocks brought nothing. She waited until the game was over, at which point she renewed her efforts and finally called building superintendent, Win Scheinblum. Scheinblum opened the door to find Bronson's body on the floor, not far from his TV set. "Tales from the Crypt" was blaring in the background. It was evident that Bronson had been stabbed, but there was no sign of any weapon. It was only then that Rose Kravitz remembered the strange man and wondered whether he might have been involved.

However, just two nights after Bronson's murder, mayhem turned to madness in the form of another tragedy at Ocean Towers. None other than Herman Gertner was found lying on the busy walkway in front of the building, having apparently fallen from his balcony. He was alive, but just barely. He remained unconscious, unable to shed any light on what had happened to him, and hopes for his recovery were dim indeed.

As you might expect, when all else failed, Inspector Forsooth was called in to investigate. Forsooth went first to Herman Gertner's condo. He found the door to the outside balcony still open. The balcony had a three-foot-high protective metal railing, but several of its screws had come loose, and it wasn't sturdy enough to prevent the tragedy. Next came the Bronson murder scene. Nothing had been touched since the murder, except that the TV had been turned off and, of course, the body had been removed. A search for fingerprints had come up empty. Forsooth then proceeded to Graham Moss's apartment. Surprisingly, Moss was nothing short of ecstatic. He had just lined up a large accounting firm to lease several floors of his faltering office building, and he relished the thought that his financial problems might be solved after all.

When Forsooth then spoke to the security personnel at the front desk, they confirmed that all three men on the "foreclosure list" had been on the premises for most of the day of Bronson's murder. Jeff Carrington had been out that morning, but he returned at about 2:00 p.m. and they didn't see him afterwards. They did see Graham Moss, who left at about 7:00 p.m. for a dinner engagement. And Herman Gertner left at about 8:00 p.m. to go bowling.

Forsooth's final stop was to interview Jeff Carrington, whose apartment was the most splendid of them all. Carrington admitted that he had gotten caught up in a free-wheeling, free-spending lifestyle, but it was now time to reform. He was trying to work out suitable arrangements to pay child support on time, but he conceded that staying at Ocean Towers was probably out of the question. He did ask how Herman Gertner was doing, and it was Inspector Forsooth's sad duty to inform him that Gertner had not survived his fall.

On his way out, Forsooth ran into none other than Rose Kravitz, who admitted that some morbid fascination had made her decide to go out and gawk at the mark in the pavement where Gertner had landed. She also admitted that she wondered whether he might have been the man she saw on Saturday, right about the time that Niles Bronson was killed.

But Forsooth didn't think so. In fact, it didn't take long for him to realize that there had been a conspiracy to kill Niles Bronson—one that involved two of our three suspects. And he knew precisely how they worked together. Do you?

1) Who killed Niles Bronson?

2) What was the role of the accomplice?

3) Who killed Herman Gertner and why?

INSPECTOR FORSOOTH ANSWERS YOUR QUESTIONS

Q1–What do we know about the motive for Bronson's murder?

We have to assume that considerable ill will had built up between Bronson and one of the men being foreclosed.

Q2–Does what the man in the hallway was wearing mean anything?

Actually, it does. His attire suggests that he wasn't hiding anything on his person.

Q3–Why were the killers "lucky not to have been unmasked right away"?

All that meant is that if Rose Kravitz had gotten a better look, she might have been able to positively ID him.

Q4–Did "Tales from the Crypt" come on directly after the game, that is, on the same channel?

No, it did not. "Tales from the Crypt" was on FOX, whereas the NCAA games were on CBS.

Q5–What was the time of the fatal attack on Bronson?

Well, my previous answer actually gives something of a clue. Remember, Bronson was a big basketball fan and wouldn't have missed those games for the world.

Q6–What floor did Gertner live on?

I'm not sure of the exact floor, but there's an important inference available here, one that's quite relevant to the solution.

Q7–What kinds of repair needed to be done to Gertner's condo?

Wouldn't you know it? His balcony needed repairing. Gertner felt that it was dangerous, and it looks as though he was right.

Q8–When do they fire up the incinerator?

Well, in this day and age, Ocean Towers didn't have an incinerator. But trash disposal is a vital ingredient to this crime, that's for sure!

Q9–Why wasn't the work done on Gertner's condo?

He always felt it was because he wasn't as wealthy as some of the other occupants of the building, and therefore didn't carry as much clout.

Q10–Did it matter that Carrington's condo was the most splendid of all of them?

Actually, in a curious way, that fact is a nice little clue, once you think about the various factors that can make an ocean-front condo splendid.

Q11–Is there an exit to the building that doesn't go by the security personnel?

No, there isn't.

Q12–Was the murder weapon dropped down an incinerator shaft?

Great question! The incinerator part has already been covered, but the shaft is a great place to look. Remember, though, the garbage area in the basement was thoroughly inspected, and they didn't come up with a murder weapon.

Can you solve the mystery?

Solution on page 78.

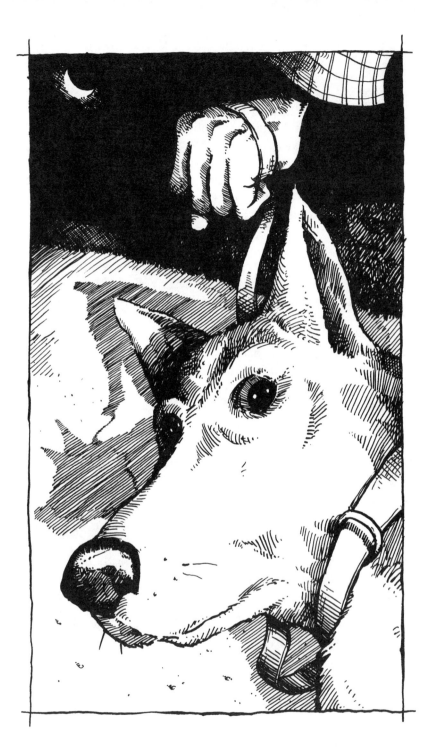

A TRAIL OF TWO CITIES

EVERYTHING ABOUT MELBA HOOGSTRATTEN'S DEATH was suspicious, from the method to the timing. Melba was a professor of English at the University of Portland, a position she had held for many years. But even a tenured professor's salary wasn't enough to satisfy her expensive lifestyle, so she established a part-time venture that had years of glory but may have led to her undoing.

The venture was a door-to-door bookselling operation called BooksAmerica. The company's approach, as developed by Melba, was to have its salespeople canvass homeowners and obtain order lists, typically among books that weren't as well publicized as the best-sellers you'd find at the major chains. BooksAmerica would then buy in bulk to satisfy those orders, which were fulfilled directly from publishers' warehouses. This way, the company obtained books at low prices and never had to worry about carrying inventory or paying for retail space. Meanwhile, publishers were delighted to get at least something for their warehouse merchandise. BooksAmerica had started with a sales force of three people and now had several hundred in its fold. Everybody was happy.

Er, not quite everybody. Things took a dark turn in the year before Melba's death. Clyde Finch, who had been the venture's very first door-to-door salesman working for Melba, didn't feel he was sharing in the company's profitability, and he threatened to set up his own organization, raiding much of BooksAmerica's sales force in the process by offering them more generous commissions. What made the situation especially difficult was that Finch had just been diagnosed as having pancreatic cancer: Although still mobile and seemingly healthy, his doctors had given him no more than five months to live. Monte Trowbridge, Melba's lawyer and himself a partner in the book venture, suggested that Finch had decided to be spiteful to Melba as his one final act in life.

The other main partner of BooksAmerica was Esther Pogue, a colleague of Melba's at the university and an avid book reader. She was more sympathetic than Melba regarding Finch's unfortunate plight, but she was also distressed at his fiendish plot. The whole matter was extremely delicate, to be sure, and Pogue suggested that they call a meeting to discuss the future of the company.

The tension was particularly high in this meeting, in no small part because of Melba's conflicting attitudes. On the one hand, she was trying to pull away from the day-to-day operations of the company. She was entering a sabbatical year, and in a few weeks she would be teaching at another university, far away. Naturally she was going to be visited periodically by those close to her, but she knew she needed a breath of fresh air.

On the other hand, Melba was understandably reluctant to lose any control of the business, especially if it wasn't on her own terms. Although the minutes of this fateful meeting were not available, a photograph of the main participants was, and that photograph later turned out to play an important role in the investigation.

Melba's death was a classic hit-and-run. The "accident" took place at night, while Melba was walking Foxy, her faithful German shepherd. A car sideswiped her from behind, and she was thrown to the ground along the side of the road. Foxy's frantic barking alerted one of Melba's neighbors, but by the time help arrived Melba had lost consciousness, and she never recovered.

An investigation of the prime suspects in the case revealed that not everyone could account for precisely where they were on the night of the murder. However, one alibi soon turned up out of nowhere. A man who lived in the same general area as Melba had his interest piqued when the newspapers released the now-infamous photograph of the principals (which, to review, were Melba, her advisor Monte Trowbridge, fellow professor Esther Pogue, and door-to-door salesman Clyde Finch).

The witness immediately called the authorities and advised that a solicitor had stopped by his house at almost precisely the time that Melba was killed, and that he was definitely the same man as in the photograph. The witness also noted that the solicitor seemed perfectly calm as he went about his business—not the sort of reaction you'd expect from a murderer. Finally, the witness said he didn't notice any marks on the car, although he admitted that it was too far away for a good inspection.

On the subject of possible stains, another surprise witness was an attendant at a nearby gas station, who swore that Monte Trowbridge had stopped by the station that night, at what turned out to be just minutes after Melba was run down. According to the attendant, the way the light of his service station shone down, he was able to get a very good look at the right portion of Trowbridge's front bumper, and swore that it was devoid of any markings. For his part, Trowbridge insisted that he had been with a client that night, and that he was completely innocent.

Esther Pogue noted that although people can sometimes make questionable eyewitnesses, dogs are more reliable. The reason she thought that important is that a day after the murder, she stopped by Melba's neighbor's house, where Foxy the German shepherd was being kept. As all who were present noted, the dog was completely friendly to Esther, even though her car was in plain sight. It was Pogue's opinion that Foxy would have reacted differently had he recognized her car as the murder vehicle.

Despite these various alibis, it was indeed possible to identify the murderer of Melba Hoogstratten. That, as you must surely know, is your very next task.

1) Which one of the suspects killed Melba Hoogstratten?

2) Indicate why the other suspects couldn't possibly have committed the crime.

INSPECTOR FORSOOTH ANSWERS YOUR QUESTIONS

Q1–Was Melba killed before or after she left for her sabbatical?

That's the remarkable part about this mystery. We don't know the answer to this question, yet we can solve the murder anyway!

Q2–Who stood to benefit from Melba's death?

Presumably any of the principals in the firm would see his or her share increased if something happened to Melba.

Q3–Was Melba going to a place where they drive on the left side of the road?

She sure was. To England, in fact. (Hence the "Trail of Two Cities" title.)

Q4–Did the gas station attendant really see Monte Trowbridge?

You know, I can't say with complete certainty that he did. But we have to take his testimony at face value.

Q5–Could Esther have been driving a different car the night of the murder?

The car itself was the same, let's just say that.

Q6–Was the doctor's diagnosis regarding Clyde Finch correct?

Yes, sorry to say, it was correct.

Q7–Could Clyde Finch still drive despite his cancer?

Yes, he could. He can't be ruled out for that reason alone.

Q8–On what side of the street was the victim walking her dog?

If it was the U.S., she was on the right side. If it was the U.K., she was on the left. Simple as that.

Q9–The alibi provided by the neighbor described the attorney as a solicitor, an English term for lawyer. Why the difference in terms?

Ah, the question I've been waiting for. The answer is that the term "solicitor" would indeed refer to an attorney in the U.K., but would refer to something else in the United States.

Q10–Are dogs color blind?

It is widely believed that they are, but in reality they can distinguish between certain colors, such as red from blue, for example.

Q11–Was Clyde Finch alive when Melba was killed?

Not if she was in England! (It may seem unlikely, but there is a strong clue that might lead you to this important conclusion.)

Q12–Are there any issues with taking a dog to England?

There sure are. England is totally devoid of rabies, and they take special precautions to make sure that the disease is never transported into the country.

Can you solve the mystery?

Solution on page 89.

TIMING IS EVERYTHING

THE CASE STARTED OUT AS A ROBBERY but ended up as a homicide. On the face of it, that's not the strangest combination in the world. But in this case the person who was robbed wasn't the person who was murdered!

Early one Saturday morning, in the country town of Cedarville, a man named Buford Huxley reported that his tool shed had been broken into. The shed was secured by an ordinary combination lock that had been cleanly severed, probably with a pair of bolt cutters. The shed was located right outside Huxley's barn, and was where he kept all sorts of gardening tools—rakes, hoes, and the like. But most important of all was that he kept a set of hunting rifles there, and one of them was missing. That item was of particular interest to Inspector Forsooth upon his arrival that morning.

Forsooth knew something that Huxley might not have known. What Forsooth knew was that a man named James Hooligan, who lived about 30 minutes away, had been murdered just the night before by a rifle shot that came through the window of his home. And that set the stage for an interesting exchange.

Shortly after Forsooth arrived at Huxley's place, Muriel Huxley came out to the barn screaming, "Did you hear what happened?!" She had been listening to an all-news radio station while doing some gardening, and had heard the account of the murder. When she saw Forsooth, she backed off a bit, and he assumed it was because her hands and face were quite dirty: She apologized for her appearance, explaining that she had just finished planting some 300 daffodil bulbs along a stone wall behind their house. However, Forsooth wasn't too concerned with how she looked, because there was more to this story than met the eye.

Buford Huxley seemed strangely self-conscious upon hearing of Hooligan's death. It was clear that Hooligan was no stranger to this household, and the ties grew deeper as the investigation progressed. For one, the murder weapon was discovered in a wooded area about halfway between the Huxley and Hooligan residences. It was Huxley's missing rifle, all right, and ballistics tests confirmed that it was the source of the fatal shots. Separately, police uncovered a pair of slightly rusty bolt cutters not far from the rifle. Huxley admitted that the gun was his, but denied any part in the shooting. However, the Huxleys had to own up to some crucial and somewhat embarrassing facts upon further questioning.

According to Muriel Huxley, James Hooligan had been blackmailing her husband and two other men, Edgar Plotz and Dinky Martinez, for their participation in a kickback scheme several years before, when her husband worked for Acme Construction Company: Plotz and Martinez had given Huxley kickbacks in return for Huxley selecting their then-struggling roofing company as a major subcontractor on projects spearheaded by Acme. Buford Huxley now worked with Plotz and Martinez in their own concrete-pouring venture, and part of the Huxley barn had been converted into an office for that venture. Hooligan had managed to figure out that the seed money for this new enterprise had come illegally.

Huxley at first denied the plot, but he conceded that he had received a threatening letter from Hooligan just days before. He also said that it was only a coincidence that the shed had been locked in the first place. He said he had gotten into an argument with his wife and obtained a lock so that she couldn't access her precious gardening tools—the rifles were the last things on his mind! He acknowledged that his two business partners were the only other people who even knew about the lock, but he was quick to add that he alone knew the combination.

The night of Hooligan's death, Huxley had held a meeting with his "co-conspirators," Plotz and Martinez. The subject, of course: What to do about the blackmailing. Plotz had arrived at 8:45; Martinez at 9:00. The meeting lasted for about an hour, with no specific plan but a lot of anger and fear all around. Huxley admitted that his two friends had talked about giving Hooligan some "concrete boots," but he didn't take their bluster very seriously. Huxley also said that he had gone back to his house after the meeting. He assumed that the others had left immediately and hadn't come back, but he admitted that he wasn't sure. However, he could confirm that the lock was quite intact when he left the meeting.

The coroner determined that James Hooligan had died sometime the prior night, but it wasn't possible to pinpoint the time of death any more than that. One potentially helpful detail came from one of Hooligan's neighbors, who had been walking her dog at about 10:30. She reported that a light was on in Hooligan's downstairs bathroom, but as she walked by, that light went off. Interestingly, Hooligan's body was found in the downstairs den, whose window was right next to the bathroom window. The shot that killed Hooligan had been fired from the outside, as evidenced by a shattered window pane and some glass fragments found in the den. When investigators arrived the next morning, the den light was still on, and the bathroom light was still off.

Dinky Martinez—who, despite his name, was a strong, stocky fellow—said he returned to his home at just before midnight, a time his wife confirmed. When asked what he did after the meeting broke up, he said that he had gone out to a neighborhood bar to shoot, er, play some pool. In fact, he had told his wife he'd been playing pool all night, to conceal the true nature of his business.

Edgar Plotz, the ringleader of the embezzlement scheme, claimed he had gone directly home after the meeting, arriving there at about 10:30. Because he lived alone, there was no one who could corroborate his story. He added that he didn't know a rifle from a bulb planter, but his lawyer cut him off before he could say more; now that the kickbacks were common knowledge, Plotz needed all the counsel he could get.

As for Huxley, he admitted that his wife was asleep when he got in after the meeting, so she couldn't vouch for him, but he insisted he didn't go anywhere.

Well, are you ready? Here are your questions:

1) Who killed James Hooligan?

2) Explain the key elements of timing in this case.

3) What was the missing piece of evidence that tied the murderer to the crime?

INSPECTOR FORSOOTH ANSWERS YOUR QUESTIONS

Q1–If the murder occurred after 10:30, would that implicate Dinky Martinez?

Yes, it sure would. Everyone else seems to have alibis for that time period, with the possible exception of Buford Huxley.

Q2–What time of year did the murder take place?

Presumably it was in the late fall, because Muriel Huxley was struggling to get all her daffodil bulbs planted before the ground froze. But the precise time of year isn't important.

Q3–Was the light hit by a shot from the rifle?

No, it wasn't. The only shots went through the window of the adjacent den. But knowing why the light went out would be very helpful regarding the timing of this case. Remember the title!

Q4–Was the murder related to the embezzlement?

Only indirectly. Sorry to be vague, but that's a clue in and of itself.

Q5–Would it have been possible for Buford Huxley to have gone to Hooligan's house without his wife knowing?

Absolutely. She was sound asleep.

Q6–Could Muriel have cut the lock after the meeting ended?

No, for the same reason as the answer to #5 above.

Q7–Could Buford Huxley have cut the lock himself, to make it look as though someone was framing him?

It is entirely possible, although there is no evidence to back that up. Wouldn't that be clever?

Q8–Was the lock the same one bought by Huxley?
Yes, it was. Great question, though.

Q9–Was the murder actually announced on the radio?
It sure was. Muriel was entirely legit.

Q10–Had Plotz ever been inside the tool shed?
It sure looks that way, judging by his comment about the rifle and the bulb planter. As for when he might have been inside, well, that's something that your supersleuth abilities should figure out.

Q11–Was the neighbor certain about the time the light went out?
Positive.

Q12–Why were the bolt cutters rusty?
Because they had been outside longer than you might have thought.

Can you solve the mystery?

Solution on page 88.

THE PIANO REQUITAL

As GILBERT VON STADE PERFORMED, there wasn't an aficionado in the house who didn't marvel at his mastery of the keyboard. Von Stade was playing Chopin's Etude in G-flat, Opus 10, No. 5, a most challenging piece by anyone's standards, even for a world-class pianist such as von Stade. The piece wasn't particularly long, as a number of performers were being showcased that night in a concert to benefit the city's sagging Foundation for the Arts. Yet it was a spellbinding few minutes.

When his work was done, von Stade got up from the piano to acknowledge a raucous standing ovation, which had become the norm at his performances. He was loved by virtually all who followed the music world; whereas other musicians of his talent tended to be aloof, he was known for being gracious and generous with his time. He took delight in the crowd, and always mingled after his concerts. But there was to be no mingling on this particular night. Against the backdrop of the applause, von Stade suddenly froze up and fell to the stage. The curtain was closed and the show came to a temporary halt. Gilbert von Slade would never regain consciousness.

At first, no one suspected foul play. Gilbert von Stade was a fairly old man, after all, and most everyone in the audience assumed that he had suffered a heart attack. Yet the autopsy would later reveal that his death was anything but natural. Traces of the rare but deadly batrachotoxin were found in his system, and had surely been responsible for his death. It was murder, all right, but it remained to determine just who could have committed such a dastardly deed.

It turned out (surprise, surprise) that there was more to the decedent's true character than was ever seen by his adoring public. As is all too often the case within the highest echelon of musical talent, von Stade was an extremely demanding person to work with, and his own search for perfection often victimized those around him. Many thought him hypocritical for basking in the public glory of his music in the wake of exhausting practice sessions in which he had bullied and badgered everyone in sight.

Perhaps because of von Stade's pre-eminence, there was considerable friction within the group of musicians performing that night. Two younger pianists, Heinrich Albertson and Vivien Frechette, were also on the evening program, and were extremely eager to prove themselves. Albertson had come on before von Stade, and had given an absolutely flawless rendition of another Chopin etude: C-Major, Opus 10, No. 1. Frechette, on the other hand, was scheduled to play immediately following von Stade, but her performance was delayed by the onstage tragedy. In fact, some of those backstage had qualms about continuing the concert under the circumstances. Stage manager Sophia Brightwell, a frequent target of von Stade's tirades, tried to convince Frechette that it would be inappropriate for her to play, but Frechette would have nothing of it. She reminded everyone that von Stade was a professional, and always lived up to the standard that the show must go on.

No one doubted that with von Stade out of the way, Albertson and Frechette had a better chance of success in their own musical careers. However, they certainly weren't the only suspects in the murder, for the rivalry had extended to the people in all of their lives, even if these very people had made a special effort that evening to heal all past wounds.

Marla Albertson, Beatrice von Stade, and Samuel Frechette never completely took to their positions as musicians' spouses. They were still very much in love with their respective mates, but they weren't necessarily attuned to their every note, so to speak. Marla Albertson was especially out of the loop, being unable to read sheet music, much less play it, but she had many other talents. One was cooking, and that night she organized a pre-concert dinner, full of special culinary treats. She prepared frog's-leg appetizers, and encouraged others to make their own contributions. Samuel Frechette brought some homemade bread and Beatrice von Stade whipped up some linguine with pesto sauce. These offerings were joined by those from many other performers and their families, as the invitees included several dozen musicians who would play that night, not just the pianists.

Although everyone applauded Marla for her initiative, the food selections weren't of universal appeal. Some of the musicians had no appetite because of pre-concert nerves, while others were reluctant to get too adventurous with their food choices while dressed in white tie. Among the pianists, only Gilbert von Stade was willing to handle greasy foods such as the frog's legs, but he made a special point of thoroughly washing his hands in the backstage men's room. On the subject of von Stade's food choices, a curious recollection of the evening's emcee, Walter Penwinkle, was that von Stade had garlic on his breath when he collapsed—on his dying breath, at that. Penwinkle and Sophia Brightwell had been the first people to rush to the stricken artist's aid, albeit in a futile cause.

After von Stade's death, the concert was delayed, but it resumed just minutes later with Vivien Frechette at the keyboard, playing Chopin's Etude in E-Flat Minor, Opus 10, No. 6. The piece was slow and melancholy, if not downright mournful, a perfect choice under the circumstances. Then, in a tribute to von Stade, Frechette astonished all the spectators by playing the precise piece von Stade had played earlier. She, too, got a rousing ovation.

Some days later, Inspector Forsooth was called in to unravel the mystery of just what happened during that ill-fated concert. He paid a visit to the stage where von Stade had fallen, and took time to survey the men's room in the back, where von Stade had washed his hands. There he found soap, toothpaste, mouthwash, some Breath-Assure tablets, and even a vial of DMSO, which Sophia Brightwell said von Stade used to take for his arthritis, before tiring of its side effects. Forsooth realized that the telling proof behind the von Stade killing might be hard to come by, but now he knew where to look.

1) Who killed Gilbert von Stade?

2) What was the method, and why did it work? Please be specific!

INSPECTOR FORSOOTH ANSWERS YOUR QUESTIONS

Q1–What is batrachotoxin?
Batrachotoxin is best known as the poison used by some South American tribes to coat their hunting arrows. The poison comes from the secretions of a certain species of tree frog. The natives would dip their arrows into the frog secretions, so even if the arrows didn't cause fatal wounds, the batrachotoxin would. (Not my style, but that's life in the jungle for you.)

Q2–Did Samuel Frechette bring garlic bread to dinner?
Nice try, but no. He brought plain bread.

Q3–How could a food poison get specifically to von Stade if the non-musicians were eating some of everything?
Good question. I haven't the foggiest idea how that would be possible.

Q4–Does the linguine have garlic in it?
The linguine doesn't have any garlic in it, but the pesto sauce is loaded with it. However, there is a pretty good clue that this didn't kill von Stade.

Q5–Are the pieces played by the pianists relevant?
Yes, they are all relevant.

Q6–What were the unwanted side effects of DMSO?
Nice question. The answer is that von Stade detested the fact that DMSO left him with a garlicky taste in his mouth! (Yes, that's an actual side effect, and it was especially intolerable for von Stade, who liked to mingle with his adoring fans.)

Q7–Does Frechette play with gloves?

No, none of them played with gloves. Another nice question, though!

Q8–Could the pianist who played before him have put the poison onto the keys?

No, that would have been extremely difficult to do, because he was in plain view of the audience the whole time. We have to assume the poison was placed there just before the show began.

Q9–What was so difficult about von Stade's piece?

Ah, I was hoping you would ask. The answer is that the piece is more difficult because it's harder for the fingers to move around on keys that are smaller!

Q10–Did everyone know what piece of music von Stade was playing that night?

Certainly all the musicians did, and everyone involved with the show did.

Q11–Could the toxin have been absorbed by the skin?

Sure could, if mixed with DMSO. One of the properties of DMSO is that it is readily absorbed through the skin, and in its liquid form is capable of carrying other compounds right along with it.

Q12–Is it possible that the victim was killed by accident, and that one of the other musicians was the actual target?

It's quite possible, and it's a great question. However, that wasn't the case, and it's our job to show how we know that.

Can you solve the mystery?

Solution on page 83.

THE VALENTINE'S DAY MASSACRE

IT WAS ONLY AFTER RUDY MARCUS was killed that his community got a full taste of what his life was really like. Marcus seemed like your average, everyday, straight-laced, white-collar type. A CPA by training, he worked at the Ernst Brothers accounting firm, and by all indications had done quite well for himself.

He had the usual trappings—a nice car and a well-groomed house in the suburbs—all in keeping with his solid-citizen image. But there wasn't much flair to Rudy. Businesswise, Rudy's customers didn't hire him because of his imagination; they hired him for the decimal-point precision with which he approached life. At home, there hadn't been a Mrs. Marcus on the scene for several years. Most people figured she had simply gotten bored.

However, within days of the discovery of Rudy's body, the entire picture changed. One of his neighbors, a Mrs. Cecily Wheelock, revealed that Rudy Marcus was in fact a closet Romeo, a prim accountant by day but a freewheeling bon vivant by night. He was having dalliances with no fewer than three women at the time of his death, each one claiming to be Rudy's real girlfriend. Those three became the focus of an extensive murder investigation.

Fittingly, Rudy had been killed on Valentine's Day, and the murder scene was consistent with a classic crime of passion. Rudy's body lay on the kitchen floor with a knife in his back. The murder weapon was one of his own kitchen knives, which had been taken from its usual resting place on the magnetic rack. It appeared that someone had stabbed Rudy the Romeo when his back was turned. From the absence of a struggle, it was assumed that Rudy knew whoever had murdered him.

The first of Rudy's mistresses to emerge was Cornelia Devane, who worked at the Estée Lauder counter at the nearby Bloomingdale's. Ms. Devane said she had been seeing Rudy for over a year, and was shocked to find out that there could have been other women in his life. But as she reflected on their relationship, she realized that his availability was sporadic. She had always chalked his busy schedule up to work-related matters, but now she knew better.

Then there was Daphne Nagelson, who had met Rudy the old-fashioned way—as a tax client. She said she was absolutely convinced that Rudy loved her the most, and to prove it she brought out an emerald brooch he had given her for Valentine's Day. Rudy had bought the brooch while in South America a few months before.

The third of Rudy's girlfriends was Mary Stahl, the only one of the three who was married. She also happened to be a city councilwoman, a highly visible role. Yet no one around her knew of her relationship with Rudy. One interesting aspect of the case, which Stahl shed light on, was that Rudy had been in California on a business trip for several days prior to his murder. Originally he was supposed to have returned on the 12th, but his client needed more help than he had planned, so he didn't return until the 13th—just one day before he was killed.

Some of the investigators wrinkled their eyebrows upon hearing that little nugget. Apparently they figured that their dead little Casanova might have had something going in other ports as well, but that was never substantiated. Mary Stahl confirmed that Rudy had been thinking about her during his trip, as she brought out a gold necklace he had bought for her while he was away.

It turned out that Rudy had prevailed upon Cornelia Devane to visit his house periodically while he was gone. Her main task was to water the plants, but he also wanted her to turn some lights on and off to thwart any potential burglars, and even to watch TV to give the house a "lived-in" look. Devane said she had done that same routine many times in the past, and expressed some feeling that she was being taken for granted. Rudy didn't call her while he was gone. However, he had unexpectedly stopped by her workplace on Valentine's Day to give her a present—a red silk scarf.

Daphne Nagelson told the police that she and Rudy had gone out to see the movie *Bed of Roses* the night before his death, and she produced the ticket stubs to prove it. Cecily Wheelock, the snoopy neighbor, said that Daphne had stopped by Rudy's house earlier on the 13th, and she didn't deny it. But she did deny having gone inside, saying that she just stopped by to drop off her Valentine present for Rudy. Mrs. Wheelock confirmed that Daphne had a little smile on her face when she left the house.

According to the "rotation" that seemed to be developing, that left Mary Stahl as Rudy's companion on the fateful night of February 14th, and, sure enough, she admitted that they, too, had gone to see a movie. When pressed as to the title, she stammered *Dead Man Walking*, not liking the irony of the title one bit. The movie was her treat, so she also had ticket stubs to present, which indicated to the authorities that Rudy was still alive until at least 9:30 p.m., when the movie ended. The coroner had already estimated the time of death as being between 8:00 p.m. and 11:00 p.m., based on the preliminary examination of such factors as rigor mortis and eye fluids. So Rudy clearly didn't live very long after the movie. Stahl also admitted that she left a message on Rudy's answering machine the night before he came home. The police located that very message on the machine.

Just when it appeared that the investigation was at a standstill, Inspector Forsooth noted that based solely on the evidence they already had, there was strong reason to believe that one particular woman in Rudy's life had found out about at least one of the others. When the authorities went back to confront that woman, a confession resulted. Your job is to figure out who confessed.

1) Who killed Rudy Marcus?

2) Rudy's personality played a role in his demise, in two distinctly different ways. Name them.

3) The testimony of two particular people would prove very helpful in bringing the guilty party to justice. Which two?

INSPECTOR FORSOOTH ANSWERS YOUR QUESTIONS

Q1–Is it proven that Mary and Rudy stayed for the whole movie?

They could have left early, but I believe they stayed for the whole thing.

Q2–Since Cornelia was housesitting for Rudy, did she intercept Mary's message on the answering machine?

We have to assume that if Cornelia was in the house, she heard the message, because he had an answering machine, not voice mail.

Q3–Did the gifts have anything to do with the murder?

They sure did, but not in the way you might think.

Q4–Which of the presents Rudy gave was the most valuable?

The emerald brooch was the most valuable, followed by the gold necklace. The red silk scarf was a distant third.

Q5–Was there any perfume scent noticed around the body?

There was a vague scent of perfume around the house, but it wasn't concentrated around the body. Sorry!

Q6–Did the police talk to Mary Stahl's husband?

No, they didn't. Actually, one of the questions asks for two witnesses who might be helpful. I can tell you right now that only one of them is named in the text, so Mr. Stahl is a good guess for the other. Alas, he's not the one.

Q7–How do you know that Daphne only went in the vestibule?

We have to take her word on that. Besides, she was only there a second or two, as Cecily Wheelock could confirm.

Q8–What was Daphne's gift? Was Rudy home when she delivered it?

I don't know what Daphne's gift was, and it really doesn't matter. But I can say that Rudy wasn't home when she delivered it. And his absence turns out to be extremely important in reaching the solution.

Q9–Where in the United States did the murder take place?
Believe it or not, it doesn't really matter. But we can assume from the language in the text that it took place outside of California, and that is important!

Q10–Is the fact that Rudy is an accountant significant?
Yes. He made a living out of reducing people's taxes, including his own. Income tax, state tax, sales tax—he hated them all. And that, believe it or not, is a big clue.

Q11–Was Cornelia angry at Rudy for not calling her while he was away?
Perhaps, but his failure to do so is good for her in a different sense, which is explained in the solution.

Q12–Where was Rudy when the package was delivered?
Rudy was not home when a particular package was delivered. (I hope that's not misleading!)

Can you solve the mystery?

Solution on page 90.

WHERE THERE'S A WILL

MARION WEBSTER WAS ONE OF THE MOST eccentric people ever to walk the planet. To him, communication was a game, to be played for personal amusement and nothing else. And when he died, everyone else was left to explain exactly what had happened. It wasn't easy.

The occasion was the 35th birthday party of Webster's eldest daughter, Laura. Each of his six children was able to make it home for the late-September festivities. Webster had three sons—Eugene, Herbert, and Biff—and three daughters—Laura, Gwen, and Dorothy. All were grown up, but none as yet had started families of their own, a fact that displeased Webster tremendously. As the family patriarch and himself a retired widower, he felt it was his role to push his children in every imaginable way, even if the results didn't always match his expectations. Unfortunately, he used his own will to reward or penalize his children's efforts. It was a fatal mistake.

Instead of simply dividing his estate equally, Webster had designated that each child would receive something consistent with his or her own interests. For example, Herbert, a struggling stockbroker, was to receive the bulk of his father's stock portfolio; Gwen, a budding socialite, was to receive a diamond necklace that had belonged to Webster's own mother. Dorothy, a librarian, was to receive Webster's extensive book collection. And so on.

The birthday weekend was filled with tension. At various times during their brief stay at Webster's Florida retreat, each of the children was summoned into the study to talk about their father's plans to reconfigure his will. The study was an imposing room, with a large oak desk in the middle and three of the four walls taken up by shelves housing his remarkable collection of reference works. It could be said that Webster's children lived in fear of their father. But tension gave way to tragedy early Sunday afternoon, when Marion Webster was found dead at his desk, the victim of a single gunshot wound to the chest.

As is so often the case, Inspector Forsooth wasn't called in until after the initial investigation had failed. One of the reasons for that failure was that none of the six children had much to say about Webster's plans with his will. Said Biff, "Everything that Dad did or said was misinterpreted, unless you knew him awfully well. Me, I was born on April Fool's Day. Maybe I learned early that things aren't always what they seem."

What was known is that the murder occurred in the early afternoon, following lunch. Gwen had made the lunch, and Laura had prepared the dessert. After lunch, Laura, Dorothy, and Herbert were outside by the pool when they heard a shot ring out. They rushed into the study and found nothing except their father's dead body. The other family members then turned up in short order. But if anyone saw anything of great importance, they weren't saying so. As if this wasn't frustrating enough, no murder weapon turned up, even though the investigators searched the rest of the house very carefully.

The only real evidence was a piece of paper found on Webster's desk that seemed to shed light on his intentions with his children. But the note contained only cryptic phrases:

I have decided to "rearrange" a portion of my will.

Bond portfolio is satisfactory—generates income.

Plan to decrease Gwen's inheritance will be put on ice.

Herb/pasta salad was commendable, and deserving
      of recognition. But a disappointment after that.

Finally, I've decided that book donations will be
      limited, but funding for libraries will increase.

      (I'm sorry that signs got crossed.)

Inspector Forsooth, after getting used to Webster's strange method of communication, was able to solve the case and obtain a confession. He was also able to determine what happened to the murder weapon by concluding that the killer must have returned to the crime scene during a lull in the first, sloppy investigation. With that in mind, here are your questions:

1) Who killed Marion Webster?

2) Where was the murder weapon hidden after the crime?

3) Which of the children was Webster going to treat harshly in his revised will? (One of them is the killer!)

INSPECTOR FORSOOTH ANSWERS YOUR QUESTIONS

Q1–Why is "rearrange" in quotes?
Because "rear range" is the same thing as "back burner," meaning that some of the will was being left unchanged for now.

Q2–Does the "Herb" in Herb/pasta salad refer to Herbert?
Yes it does.

Q3–Was Webster referring to lunch when he said "a disappointment"?
No!

Q4–Was Webster the sort of guy who would change his will over a stupid dessert?
You never know with Webster, but one has to believe that he wasn't that strange.

Q5–Is there a distinction between a stock portfolio and a bond portfolio?
There sure is. The bond portfolio was not going to Herbert the stockbroker.

Q6–Why does Webster's note say "Bond portfolio is satisfactory—generates income"?
Because the name of the person who deserves the income is right there, if you look hard enough.

Q7–What was Eugene to inherit?
I think that question was just answered!

Q8–Is it important that Biff was born on April Fool's Day?
In an incredibly obscure way, yes.

Q9–Did they have pasta salad for lunch?
There is no evidence to suggest that they did.

Q10–Was Herb's childhood commendable?
Apparently it was, and that's what Webster was trying to communicate. As I indicated in my prior answer, whether they actually had pasta salad for lunch is anyone's guess.

Q11–Does "signs" refer to signs of the zodiac?
Yes!

Q12–How many "losers" were there in Webster's revised will?
There were three. And remember, every one of Webster's children is accounted for in his cryptic notes!

Can you solve the mystery?

Solution on page 94.

THE OVERHEAD SMASH

IT WAS NO ORDINARY U.S. OPEN, that's for sure. This one had a special excitement to it, what with political intrigue in the second week and some breathtaking tennis on the final weekend. But Manny Heitz never made it that far.

Heitz's body was discovered on Friday afternoon during the first week of the tournament. He was working as a linesman throughout the event, and had been scheduled to work two matches on that fateful day—an early-round singles match in the stadium at 11 a.m. and then a late-afternoon doubles match on the grandstand court. But when he didn't show up for the second match, tournament officials sent someone over to his house. Heitz's body was found in the kitchen of his home, not far from the tennis stadium. He was wearing his official U.S. Open outfit.

Heitz had been struck on the head, and the murder weapon wasn't especially difficult to find: His Wilson T2000 tennis racquet lay by his side, the top of its frame stained with blood. Closer examination revealed that there were several strands of hair stuck to the blood, hair that turned out to be Heitz's. The room bore the signs of a struggle, and it was therefore surmised that the death may have been accidental, in the sense that the perpetrator might have struck Heitz without intending to kill him. Either way, the coroner estimated that the time of death was between 12:00 and 2:00 in the afternoon. The autopsy also revealed two separate blows to Heitz's right temple, one of which may have been enough to have knocked him out, the other of which was presumed to have been fatal.

Interviews with other linespeople who worked that first match revealed that no one had any recollection that anything was wrong. However, it turned out that none of them really knew Manny Heitz in any real sense. They were focusing on calling their own lines, and not much else.

Of the people who actually knew the victim, one of the last to see him alive was Ernie Welch, who owned a sporting goods store in the area. Apparently Heitz had stopped by

Welch's store early in the morning on the day of his death to buy a few tennis-related items—wrist bands, a pair of sneakers, and a couple of pairs of socks. Heitz wanted to look his best when he was on the stadium court.

According to Ernie Welch, the match that Heitz was going to be involved with at 11:00 was a big one, as early-rounders go: Tracy Molotov of the Soviet Union versus Chris de la Harpe of South Africa. The match was especially meaningful to Heitz because one of his frequent doubles partners, Wayne Melanson, was Molotov's agent, while another occasional partner, Roger Dant, was de la Harpe's cousin. Each of them had actually tried to bribe Heitz to make calls that were favorable to the player of their choice! At first Heitz thought they were joking, but Welch remembered warning him that he was underestimating their fanaticism.

What happened in the match was truly bizarre. Molotov, the favorite, was beaten by de la Harpe in one of the day's major upsets, in part because the side linesman called Molotov's patented slice serves wide on a couple of crucial break points, thereby taking away one of his most potent weapons. Molotov was absolutely convinced that the balls in question had skidded off the tape, and was livid when the umpire refused to overrule (as they so often decline to do). Molotov eventually lost his cool, and with it the match.

Another friend of the victim, a woman named Janet Stringfellow, had been in the stadium for that match. She later said that the emotions during those line-call arguments were so strained that she joked to a friend, to her later regret, that Heitz would be lucky to escape with his life! But she was on the other side of the court, well up in the stadium, and was unable to see the action very closely. In fact, she said that she had trouble distinguishing the two men who were playing! Apparently the match wasn't nearly as important to Stringfellow as to some of the others. She joked that she hadn't followed the game in a while, and probably wouldn't recognize any tennis players that weren't Jimmy Connors or Bjorn Borg! She also said that she spent the afternoon at the tournament, trying to reacquaint herself with the whole tennis scene.

Upon investigating Heitz's alleged buddies Roger Dant and Wayne Melanson, some interesting facts turned up. For one, Melanson was extremely upset by Molotov's early loss, because he thought his client had a chance of breaking through all the way to the semi-finals. Melanson didn't see the de la Harpe match personally, but he admitted that early that afternoon, upon finding out about the controversy, he went to Heitz's place to confront him. However, he insisted that by the time he arrived, Heitz was already dead! Melanson left without telling anyone, fearful that someone would suspect his involvement. Investigators noted that Melanson was much bigger than Heitz, and would have had no trouble subduing him.

As for Dant, he said that he had watched the entire Molotov/de la Harpe match, and had then gone to the local public courts and picked up a game. He pointed to his scraped knee, an injury he said he incurred because the courts had not been watered recently and were therefore slippery. Dant also said he had a conversation with a woman who was admiring his "RACQUET" vanity license plate, which was easily visible because of the dark letters on the bright orange background. He said he talked to the woman for over 20 minutes before the pickup game started, and he remembered getting on the court at precisely 1:00 p.m. The authorities of course set out to confirm these various claims.

Upon piecing together all these bits of information, Inspector Forsooth was able to come up with the solution—your very next task. Here are the questions you must answer:

1) Who killed Manny Heitz? What was the murder scenario?

2) What was the crucial piece of evidence the killer tried to cover up? Why was his effort doomed to failure?

3) Let's suppose that this case came to trial. Although no one saw the crime committed except for the killer and the victim, name one person whom the prosecution would surely want to get as a witness for its side.

INSPECTOR FORSOOTH ANSWERS YOUR QUESTIONS

Q1–Is Molotov left-handed?

We can deduce that he is, yes, because his "patented slice serves" were called out on "crucial break points" by a "side linesman." Most break points in tennis arise in the so-called "ad court," where a slice serve is most effective for a left-hander because it brings the ball out wide (à la John McEnroe). However, given that Janet Stringfellow had trouble distinguishing between Molotov and de la Harpe, it follows that both of them are left-handed! (A lot of work for not much reward, wouldn't you say?)

Q2–Don't New York license plates have a white background? They do now, but they weren't always like that.

Q3–What is the significance of the clothing that the dead man had bought?

Believe it or not, one specific item that Manny Heitz purchased is a big help in tracking down the killer.

Q4–Did Heitz live close to the National Tennis Center?

Hmmm. A good question. Heitz lived about 15 minutes by car from the National Tennis Center in Flushing Meadows, but that's a highly misleading answer!

Q5–The story says that Molotov was from the Soviet Union. Isn't that out-of-date?

No, it is not. And that's a useful clue, in and of itself.

Q6–What is the average length of a men's singles match at the U.S. Open?

It is fairly uncommon for three-out-of-five-set men's matches to take less than two hours, but there is a very good reason why this particular match was shorter than what we might be accustomed to. Let's assume each set of the match took one hour. Okay?

Q7–When did New York State adopt its current license plates?

In 1976, the bicentennial year, New York made a patriotic move toward red, white, and blue plates. Prior to that time, the plates were orange with dark blue lettering.

Q8–Was Melanson angry at Heitz? Hadn't Heitz's calls cost Melanson a lot of money?

The answer to the first question is yes: He certainly was angry, at least for a while. The answer to the second question, technically, is no.

Q9–Why in the world was Heitz playing with a T2000? I thought they went out of style years ago!

You're right. They did. The Wilson T2000—the first steel racquet and for years the weapon of choice (so to speak) for one Jimmy Connors—was a revolutionary product but was also one of the worst racquets ever made! However, it was once in vogue.

Q10–Why is the sideline referred to as a "tape"?

Because the match in question was not being played on a hard court, in which case the term "line" would have sufficed.

Q11–Was Heitz wearing the new tennis shoes when he died? He sure was.

Q12–Did Heitz make it to his 11:00 match?

No, he did not. But a sleuth of your skill had figured that out already, right?

Can you solve the mystery?

Solution on page 81.

PIER FOR THE COURSE

INSPECTOR FORSOOTH'S FINAL CASE (for now) shows how dangerous it is to play with guns—especially when hard-core, aggressive corporate types are involved. The occasion of interest to us is the off-site meeting of the Fairport Firearms Company. For several years the firm's senior and middle managers had met at some unusual locales to bond, try out different management techniques, and ultimately to test the mettle of all those who attended. This time around, the group agreed to go on a hunting and fishing expedition at Lake Nineveh. It was a decision that permanently changed the company and the lives of those who worked for it.

The focus of the weekend was on three of the company's vice presidents, all of whom were extremely hungry for professional advancement: David Willoughby, the chief financial officer; Kevin Van Allen, the head of the sales division; and Paula Fine, the marketing director. Each of these three was the head of a corporate "team" for the off-site meeting. The reason this turned out to be important is that only the team leaders spent any time by themselves—everyone who worked under them was always in a group, with others to attest to their whereabouts. The three groups took turns occupying different areas of the lakeside, each of which offered its own special terrain. Although no hunting was done per se, everyone had real guns and blanks for use in the role-playing survival games that the teams were engaging in. The whole idea of the weekend was to create a primitive setting that would develop ingenuity and teamwork.

Tragedy struck at lunchtime on the second day of the meeting. Each employee had been given a box lunch containing a peanut-butter-and-jelly sandwich, potato chips, bottled water, and, finally, a caramel apple to celebrate the fall season. The only exception to the rule was senior vice president Wayne Metzger, the second-most-powerful person in the company; he was given a ham sandwich instead of the standby PB&J because of a longstanding and extremely serious allergy to

peanut oil. Metzger and company president Bart Strunk were the only two who didn't participate in the management games that morning. Instead, they located themselves on a pier that jutted out into the lake, prepared to enjoy some relaxing trout fishing. But neither one made it off the pier alive.

The first people to reach the crime scene were David Willoughby and his assistant, Sharon Sturgis. In a sense, their appearance was surprising, because just prior to the lunch break Willoughby's group had been out at Rocky Point, the most remote locale of them all. But they wanted to see how the fishing was going—and perhaps pick up a few corporate brownie points—so they headed to the pier. They saw the bodies from a distance and ran toward them. Sturgis tried in vain to revive Metzger, who had collapsed for unknown reasons. Willoughby went farther out on the pier, where Bart Strunk lay dead. Strunk had been shot twice in the chest. Willoughby noted to his assistant that the two must have just finished their lunch, as the core of Strunk's caramel apple lay beside him, still white. Metzger's sandwich was finished, but he hadn't gotten to his apple yet. The bottled water, plastic cups, and potato chip bags were strewn around the pier. Clearly the men hadn't had a chance to clean up.

The other two groups—led by Kevin Van Allen and Paula Fine—were quickly called in, and the fun and games stopped right there. Because the woods had been resounding with fake gunfire throughout the day, no one could be sure exactly where the shots that hit Bart Strunk had come from, or, for that matter, when they had been fired. But the murder weapon was eventually fished out of the lake, not far from the pier. Fittingly, Strunk had been shot by one of his firm's own guns.

The search for clues began, and a number of interesting facts turned up. Some had to do with the corporate intrigue at Fairport Firearms, such as the fact that Van Allen and Fine had a romantic relationship. They had tried to keep the relationship a secret, but they were caught red-handed on Lake Nineveh: When asked what they were doing during the time just before the discovery of the bodies, they had no choice but to admit that they had sneaked away for a romantic liaison in the woods. The two seemed embarrassed by the disclosure, but they realized that it would have looked much worse if they had been unable to account for their whereabouts. In any event, many people in the company had figured out that Van Allen and Fine had long-term plans for themselves as a couple, plans that included running Fairport Firearms one day.

The odd man out among the three vice presidents was David Willoughby, who had a particularly close working relationship with the late Wayne Metzger. Metzger, as senior vice president, apparently treated Willoughby roughly, and took full use of the corporate power he held. However, Willoughby was also fiercely loyal to Metzger, and always saw to it that Metzger's personal quirks were satisfied. He figured that if Metzger was going to be running the show at some point, it made sense to play along.

As far as the off-site meeting went, the murder investigation confirmed some basic details. First of all, because there were so many extra guns around, the murder weapon could not be pinned on any one person or team. However, it was readily determined that the group led by Paula Fine had been in the area closest to the pier for the 20 minutes or so prior to the discovery of the bodies. Sturgis added that as part of standard procedure, she had double-checked Metzger's box lunch after Willoughby's initial check and didn't notice anything wrong with it.

Inspector Forsooth surveyed the evidence and came to a surprising conclusion—that the deaths had resulted from a two-person conspiracy! More than that, there was a twist at the end, because Forsooth claimed that one of the co-conspirators had pulled a double-cross! Your job is to determine who spoiled the fun and games at Lake Nineveh. Specifically, you must answer the following questions:

1) Who killed Bart Strunk?

2) Who killed Wayne Metzger?

3) How was Metzger killed? You must be specific as to how the crime was perpetrated.

INSPECTOR FORSOOTH ANSWERS YOUR QUESTIONS

Q1–Did Metzger collapse because he ate something containing peanut oil?

That's right. It was determined that Metzger died from an allergic reaction that closed his larynx, and traces of peanut oil were found in his stomach.

Q2–Was Metzger poisoned by something in his lunch?

The answer, literally speaking, is no. But he was poisoned, all right. (Note that peanut oil isn't a poison as such, but it is considered a poison in this case, given Metzger's allergy.)

Q3–Did the bottled water or cups play an important role?

The answer is an emphatic yes. The existence of the cups was an essential part of the conspiracy, believe it or not.

Q4–From what distance was Strunk shot?

It simply wouldn't have been possible for anyone to have shot Strunk from afar, because the shots came from an almost head-on angle, eliminating the possibility that the killer had been farther down along the shore. And because of the dense woods, the shots would never have gotten through unless the killer was near the shore.

Q5–Does that mean that someone in the group closest to the pier must have fired the shot?

Absolutely. Remember, though, those groups rotated.

Q6–Which group was scheduled to have been closest to the pier after the lunch break?

Kevin Van Allen's.

Q7–Was it a coincidence that Sharon Sturgis attended to Wayne Metzger?

Not at all. The entire murder plot depended on who took care of which corpse!

Q8–How long does an allergy to peanut oil take to set in?

Not very long. Metzger probably didn't last more than 15 seconds or so.

Q9–Was it the candied apple that was laced with peanut oil? And did someone know that Metzger was going to eat Strunk's apple?

Believe it or not, the answer to both questions is a resounding yes!

Q10–Was one of the dead guys involved in the conspiracy?

Again, yes!

Q11–Did Willoughby have an alibi?

His alibi was that the apple was still white. Given that he was in a remote locale just prior to when the body was found, it appeared that he couldn't have been involved, because an apple core will turn brown fairly quickly if left out in the open.

Q12–Who died first, Strunk or Metzger?

Great question. The answer is that Strunk died first.

Can you solve the mystery?

Solution on page 85.

Answers

SOLUTION TO "THE FINAL FORECLOSURE" (page 31)

1) Who killed Niles Bronson?
Graham Moss was the killer, assisted by Herman Gertner.

2) What was the role of the accomplice?
To dispose of the murder weapon. After killing Gertner, Moss put the knife in a sheath, placed the sheath in a bag, and dropped it down the trash chute to Gertner, who was waiting on his floor, several floors below, with a basket or some such receptacle to catch it. Gertner later placed the weapon in his bowling bag so he could remove it from the building without attracting suspicion. (Note that Gertner would have been most unlikely to even temporarily survive a plunge of as much as fifteen stories, so one can infer that he lived well below Niles Bronson. Jeff Carrington and Graham Moss, on the other hand, lived above Bronson.)

Why not Carrington instead of Moss? Well, note that in his journey through the condominium complex, Inspector Forsooth spoke to the security personnel in between speaking to Moss and Carrington. Why? Because Carrington lived in a penthouse apartment (hence the splendid views), which was accessed via a different elevator bank! To get to Bronson's apartment, Carrington would have had to return to the main floor—as Inspector Forsooth did—where he would have been spotted by the ever-vigilant security folks.

By the way, we know that the building had a trash chute by the fact that Rose was taking her garbage out on a Saturday afternoon (NCAA semi-final games are played on Saturdays). It would be highly unlikely for anyone to come around picking it up on a Saturday or a Sunday, and it would also be unlikely that the garbage would remain in the hallway of such an upscale building.

Note that the description of the murder scene indicates that Bronson was killed before the beginning of the basketball game(s), because his TV was still tuned to FOX ("Tales from the Crypt"), whereas it would have been on CBS had he been alive to watch the basketball. Therefore, neither Moss nor Gertner has any alibi for that time. (I suppose Moss could have changed the channel after killing Bronson to make it look as though he was killed after the games, but Rose Kravitz's intrusion eliminates that possibility.) Finally, the fact that Moss's personal fortunes were turning around is irrelevant. He didn't find out about the accounting firm moving into his building until Monday, by which time Bronson was already dead.

3) Who killed Herman Gertner and why?

Either Gertner was trying to blackmail Moss or expose him. Either way, Gertner wasn't cooperating, and Moss decided to get rid of him, too. Case closed.

SOLUTION TO "HALLOWEEN HORROR" (page 19)

1) Who killed the ghost?

The murderer was the girl who was trick-or-treating in the cheerleader costume. She planted a poisoned Butterfinger bar in Mrs. MacDonald's candy bowl.

2) How could the killer feel confident that no one other than the intended victim would be killed by the poison?

First of all, the ghost was the next person heading to Mrs. MacDonald's house. Second, even if the ghost elected not to take the Butterfinger bar (which was clearly the best choice available), it was late in the evening, and it was unlikely that another trick-or-treater would come along. Finally, even if the candy bar had not been selected by the ghost or anyone else, Mrs. MacDonald wasn't going to eat it, just as she apparently didn't eat her taffy. You don't see many octogenarians with dentures sinking their (false) teeth into a chewy candy bar.

3) How did the killer's choice of costume play a role?

The cheerleader's costume was complete with a set of pom-

poms. (Actually, the correct term is "pompon," but it looks like a typo!) These "pom-poms" came in handy, because they enabled the cheerleader to hide the tainted Butterfinger as she reached into the candy bowl. She then buried the bar so that it wasn't completely obvious, but so that the ghost (with sharper eyes than Mrs. MacDonald) would be able to spot it. And the rest is history.

SOLUTION TO "MURDER AROUND THE CLOCK" (page 7)

1) Who killed Bruce Berringer?
The killer was Sean McGillicuddy, the milkman.

2) How can the other suspects be ruled out?
There are two ways to solve the murder—the hard way and the easy way. First off, we note that when Berringer wrote "1:30 hence," he wasn't referring to the time of the shooting; he was referring to what the position of the clocks would be 1 hour and 30 minutes hence. (As discussed in the Q&A, the "hence" meant "in the future," not "therefore.")

The hard way to solve the crime is to use semaphore code directly. At approximately 2:37 Mountain Time (the time zone in Bogusville) it would be 3:37 in Chicago, the first of the seven clocks on the wall. But if you look at the hand positions at 3:37, you'll see they are quite close to the flag positions of the letter "M" in the semaphore alphabet (right arm at a slight angle to the left, left arm almost straight out to the right).

Now apply the same logic to each of the seven clocks. At 2:37 Mountain Time it would be 10:37 in Paris, which corresponds roughly with the "I" in semaphore. And so on for Los Angeles ("L" = 1:37), Cairo ("K" = 11:37), Mexico City ("M" = 3:37), Caracas ("A" = 5:37), and New York ("N" = 4:37). The correspondences aren't all perfect (Berringer was a dying man, after all), but there is a strong match between the indicated times and letters. Together, the letters spell out "MILKMAN." Berringer was identifying Sean McGillicuddy, the milkman, as his killer.

But you didn't need to know semaphore to figure this case out. The "easy" way is to observe that Chicago and Mexico City are in the same time zone, meaning that they would signify the same letter in the semaphore alphabet! Right away we know that Berringer couldn't have been referring to Dowling or Walters (the only two suspects whose last names have seven letters), because neither name has any repeated letters. The only conclusion is that Berringer, true to his approach to life, must have been identifying his killer by using the man's profession, not his name.

Wouldn't you know that each of the five professions— CATERER, PLUMBER, MILKMAN, REFEREE, and MAITRE D'—has seven letters? However, we can rule out four of them, as follows:

Using the same logic as we used earlier for the names Dowling and Walters, the killer couldn't have been the plumber or the maître d', because each letter in those job titles is distinct. Similarly, the position of the clocks couldn't possibly be identifying the referee (four e's), or the caterer (two sets of repeated letters). "MILKMAN" was the only job that had one and only one repeated letter, spelling doom for Sean McGillicuddy.

McGillicuddy thought he had stumbled onto the perfect alibi when first questioned concerning his whereabouts at 1:30 a.m., a time when he in fact was out with several others who could vouch for him. But at interactive mysteries, we always get our man.

SOLUTION TO "THE OVERHEAD SMASH" (page 65)

1) Who killed Manny Heitz? What was the murder scenario?

Roger Dant killed Manny Heitz. Dant arrived at Heitz's residence before the 11:00 match and the two got into an argument. The result was that Dant knocked Heitz out and took his place as a linesman. (With sunglasses and a visor, the disguise was made easier. The only people who would have known the difference were too far away. Note also that Dant and Heitz were about the same size.) Heitz was left bound and gagged until after the match. When Dant returned, the two got into another struggle, one that resulted in Heitz's death.

The reason the two got into an argument in the first place was that Dant wanted Chris de la Harpe to win the tennis match. Heitz wasn't willing to be bribed, so Dant decided to take matters in his own hands—making bad calls in de la Harpe's favor to facilitate the upset.

2) What was the crucial piece of evidence that the killer tried to cover up? Why was his effort doomed to failure?

The crucial piece of evidence against Dant was that his sneakers had clay on them from the stadium court at Forest Hills. The year was 1975, and the U.S. Open was being played on clay for the first time. That year, the early men's matches were two out of three sets, not three out of five, which is why the Molotov/de la Harpe match was so short, which in turn enabled Dant to be there for the whole match and still make it to Heitz's house and then the public courts by 1:00 p.m. Also, this explains my "highly misleading" answer to Question #4, in which I note that Heitz lived 15 minutes away from the National Tennis Center at Flushing Meadows (where the U.S. Open moved in 1978). Had I wanted to be more helpful, I would have added that he lived right next to the stadium at Forest Hills! (By the way, the "political intrigue" of that particular U.S. Open was the fact that Martina Navratilova announced her defection to the United States!)

Dant realized that after he killed Heitz, he was in big trouble. He therefore scampered to the local public courts, which were also clay (technically Har-Tru, a green, granular, clay-like surface). By picking up a game, Dant found someone who could vouch for his whereabouts. He also made sure someone noticed his vanity plate. (As noted during the question-and-answer session, New York license plates were orange before the bicentennial year of 1976, when they went to a more conventional red and blue lettering on a white background.) Most important of all, Heitz was able to get Har-Tru granules on his sneakers, covering up the fact that he had been on the stadium court.

What Dant hadn't counted on was that Manny Heitz was wearing brand-new sneakers! The absence of Har-Tru granules on the soles of Heitz's sneakers proved he hadn't been at the 11:00 match after all.

3) Name one person whom the prosecution would surely want as a witness for their side.

One person who could have served as a witness for the prosecution was Tracy Molotov. He got a close look at Dant, and despite the visor and sunglasses, he would have been unlikely to forget his face!

SOLUTION TO "THE PIANO REQUITAL" (page 49)

1) Who killed Gilbert von Stade?

Vivien Frechette. She felt she was every bit von Stade's equal (as evidenced by her strong performance of the complicated piece he had chosen), but she never got anywhere near the recognition he did. That's right: Gilbert von Stade was the victim of professional jealousy.

2) What was the method, and why did it work?

Just before the beginning of the show, Frechette laced a couple of the black keys in the upper (right-hand) region of the piano with a combination of batrachotoxin and DMSO (dimethyl sulfoxide, in case you want to impress your friends). Note that she didn't have to go to South America to find the poison; it is available at various medical labs in the United States, for example. And all it took was a few drops.

As discussed in the question-and-answer session, DMSO plays a vital role because of its property of being quickly absorbed into the body. DMSO is capable of carrying other compounds into the bloodstream along with it, even if the person's only contact with the mixture is with the surface of the skin. However, one of DMSO's common side effects is that it leaves the user with a garlicky taste in his mouth! (Note: It was quite unlikely that von Stade's garlic breath came from something he ate. After all, he was in the men's room between the dinner and the performance, and he could have used any of the items there to deal with the garlic taste that he plainly disliked.)

The reason why Heinrich Albertson wasn't killed is that his piece (Etude in C-Major) uses almost no black keys, whereas von Stade's piece (Etude in G-flat) is commonly referred to as Chopin's "black key" etude, such is its emphasis on flats and sharps. Because the poisonous solution was a skimmed-on liquid, von Stade might have noticed that something was amiss, but, being the seasoned professional that he was, he evidently concluded that the show must go on.

In theory, the fact that the show went on would have boded poorly for Vivian Frechette, who followed von Stade in the evening's program. But von Stade had basically wiped the keys clean with his hands; in addition, Frechette's first piece, being slow and melancholy, was much longer than the others, which, coupled with the disruption following von Stade's death, would have given the remaining solution time to evaporate under the stage lights! These factors all but eliminated the possibility that a lethal or even toxic dosage could have made its way into her bloodstream. (Also, her first piece uses almost exclusively the white keys in the lower ranges of the keyboard, as opposed to the higher-pitched flats and sharps of the black-key etude.)

Theoretically, it was possible that someone who wasn't familiar with the music was trying to kill Heinrich Albertson instead, but the only person who was unfamiliar with sheet music was Marla Albertson; however, she was still very much in love with her husband, and had no apparent reason to do him in. And that's a wrap.

SOLUTION TO "PIER FOR THE COURSE" (page 71)

1) Who killed Bart Strunk?
David Willoughby.

2) Who killed Wayne Metzger?
Again, David Willoughby.

3) How was Metzger killed? You must be specific as to how the crime was perpetrated.
The conspiracy was between senior vice president Wayne Metzger and vice president David Willoughby. Metzger pressured Willoughby into shooting Bart Strunk so that he (Metzger) could take over the reins of the company.

But Willoughby insisted on having an alibi. He agreed to shoot Strunk just as he was finishing his caramel apple. The plan was that Metzger would then place the apple core in a cup of water—this would prevent the apple from "aging," as it would if left in the air, and would make it seem as though Strunk had been shot at a time when Willoughby wasn't in the area. Metzger agreed, the idea being that Willoughby would leave the pier area for a remote site, at which point Metzger would wait a little while before getting help, then would take the apple out of the water to misconstrue the time of the killing and provide Willoughby with an alibi.

The only wrinkle was that Willoughby, standing at a point on the shore, killed Strunk a bit too soon—on purpose! Metzger found that the apple was too big to fit in the cup of water, and he therefore hurriedly ate the rest of it himself! This is precisely what Willoughby had anticipated. He knew he had a chance to kill two birds with one stone (ultimately he felt angry at being Metzger's flunky for so many years), and he had taken the opportunity to place peanut oil on the outside of Strunk's caramel apple at its widest point—when, ostensibly, he was checking Metzger's food to make sure he had a ham sandwich instead of peanut butter and jelly. The taste of the peanut oil was obscured by the caramel, and of course Strunk consumed it without any side effects. But Metzger's intense allergy to peanut oil (a well-known and very serious condition) caused his larynx to tighten up within mere seconds of its ingestion. Metzger had time to place the apple in the water cup, but that's about it. He never made it off the pier.

The final touch was that Willoughby made sure he found the bodies first, confident that the others would be distracted by their own projects. When he arrived with Sharon Sturgis, he saw to it that she attended to Wayne Metzger, so that he could attend to Strunk. Willoughby simply removed the apple from the cup of water, thereby creating the illusion that his alibi depended on.

That's it!

SOLUTION TO "THE PRINTS OF LIGHTNESS" (page 23)

1) Who killed Oscar Delahanty?

The killer was Stan Norton, with an assist (either intentional or otherwise) from Ginger LaCroix.

First of all, Norton killed Oscar Delahanty by smothering him with a pillow. It was apparent that Delahanty must have been alive when the workmen started that morning, because his windows were closed. Ordinarily those windows would have been open at night to give the room some air—as we learned in the question-and-answer session, the house, being a landmark site, would not have been permitted to have central air conditioning. The need for fresh air would have been even greater than usual because of the chemicals used by the floor refinishers. The conclusion is that Delahanty was awakened by the noise of the jackhammer (a necessary part of the hydrant installation, because underground pipes would have to be exposed). He then closed the bedroom window and went back to sleep.

It follows that the killer must have arrived sometime after the workmen started, which was at 8:30 a.m. Therefore, Mitchell Quinn couldn't have been the killer, because he had been in the salon since 8:00.

Ginger LaCroix wasn't the killer, but for a different reason. She was also going to be let go by her boss, and had also harbored thoughts of killing him. Therefore, she started the fire! (Note that she expressed concern about the condition of the house upon hearing that her boss had died of asphyxia; at that point, however, the authorities hadn't mentioned anything about a fire.) Why Norton didn't arrive at the salon until after LaCroix is anyone's guess, but clearly the strangulation occurred before the fire! Note that we don't have enough information to conclude that there was a conspiracy between Norton and LaCroix. In fact, their separate confessions suggest they weren't working in cahoots.

2) Who wrongly confessed to the crime?

Ginger LaCroix. She honestly believed that she had killed Delahanty by setting fire to his home. However, Delahanty was already dead by the time Ginger arrived, as suggested by his inability to react to the smoke alarm. Of course, Ginger wasn't completely off the hook. She still faced an arson rap, and was lucky to avoid prosecution for attempted murder!

3) How did the coroner's report help identify the killer?

The autopsy would have revealed that Delahanty did not have any soot in his lungs, as would have been expected had he actually died of smoke inhalation. (There would also have been any number of specific indications that he had been smothered, but ruling out smoke inhalation as the cause of death was the most important autopsy finding.)

4) What was the "evidence" that was destroyed?

As Norton left Delahanty's house, he left his footprints on the back steps, which were still not completely dry because of the humid weather. However, this entire area, footprints included, was destroyed in the fire. And that's a wrap.

SOLUTION TO "TIMING IS EVERYTHING" (page 43)

1) Who killed James Hooligan?
Muriel Huxley.

2) Explain the key elements of timing in this case.

First of all, the bathroom light of Hooligan's case simply burned out; it bore no relationship to the crime! (Before you cry "foul play," let me say that this little nugget came from a real case. Unlikely, but true.)

As for the method, Muriel had cut the combination lock off a couple of days before the murder, and had replaced it with an identical-looking combination lock. Her husband never realized the change had taken place, because he didn't have any occasion to get into the cabinet in the meantime. Muriel also took the rifle out at that earlier time. She killed Hooligan prior to the meeting between her husband, Martinez, and Plotz, and she ditched the rifle in the woods, just as she had ditched the bolt cutters a couple of days before. But the extra rust on the bolt cutters suggested they might have been outside longer than just one night. A fatal mistake.

A couple of other small "timing" clues pointed Muriel's way. Remember that when she came down with the news of Hooligan's death, she had just finished planting all those daffodil bulbs. But she couldn't have been planting all that long;

it was still morning, and besides, she had just heard the radio announcement, which presumably had been mentioned many times on her all-news station. It follows that she had been doing her gardening for several days despite her being "locked out" of the shed, taking advantage of her husband's preoccupation with the kickback scheme.

3) What was the missing piece of evidence that tied the murderer to the crime?

The missing piece of evidence was the other lock—the one Muriel Huxley bought to replace the lock she cut off with the bolt cutters! (If you guessed the burned-out light bulb in Hooligan's bathroom, take credit for some good sleuthing.)

And just why did Muriel kill James Hooligan? Because she and her husband were getting along dreadfully, and she saw a way out of the marriage, the blackmailing, everything. She knew that her husband and/or his henchmen would be blamed for the crime, precisely because she had no apparent motive. Unfortunately for poor Muriel, she was now going to a place where someone else would hold the key to the lock.

SOLUTION TO "A TRAIL OF TWO CITIES" (page 37)

1) Which one of the suspects killed Melba Hoogstratten?
Esther Pogue killed Melba.

2) Indicate why the other suspects couldn't possibly have committed the crime. Be complete!

As indicated during the question-and-answer session, the alibis depend on where the murder took place. With that in mind, let's look at the alibis for Clyde Finch and Monte Trowbridge.

In Finch's case, if the murder had taken place in the U.S., the "solicitor" alibi would apply to him, because that's the term for a door-to-door salesman. But if the murder took place in the U.K., Finch would have already died! That's because, by assumption, he had only five months to live, whereas Foxy, the German shepherd, would have been quarantined for six months before being allowed to live in the U.K.—that's standard procedure to guard against a rabies outbreak, and explains why Question #12 came into the picture. Either way, Finch could not have committed the crime.

Now consider Monte Trowbridge. He could not have committed the crime in the U.S., because the gas station attendant noted that his right front bumper (where Melba would have been struck, had the hit-and-run occurred on the right side of the road) was devoid of any markings. However, had Melba been murdered in the U.K., the "solicitor" alibi would have applied to him. Either way, Monte is innocent.

Although sleuths weren't required to say anything about Esther Pogue's would-be "alibi," it was clear that the whole story about the dog didn't hold water. Evidently Pogue had her car repainted, but there is no guarantee that Foxy would have recognized it in the first place—and, in any event, the repainted car would have looked different, assuming that the shift was, say, from blue to red. (Dogs are, in fact, color blind with respect to some color combinations.)

That's it!

SOLUTION TO "THE VALENTINE'S DAY MASSACRE" (page 55)

1) Who killed Rudy Marcus?
Daphne Nagelson killed Rudy Marcus.

2) Rudy's personality played a role in his demise, in two distinctly different ways. Name them.
First, and most obviously, Rudy's philandering is what got him in trouble. Second, Rudy was a victim of the accountant in him. When he bought Mary Stahl a gold necklace in California, he had it shipped home, thereby avoiding the state

sales tax. Unfortunately for Rudy, when his business trip was delayed, the UPS delivery person arrived with his package before he was home to receive it. The delivery person left either the package or a little slip of paper (we don't really know which) in Rudy's vestibule. Whatever was left bore the markings of a California boutique, which didn't go unnoticed by Daphne when she stopped by to drop off her present to Rudy. At the time, she doubtless thought the present was for her, hence the smile on her face. When she got the emerald brooch instead, she may have been delighted to receive it, but she immediately knew that Rudy was a two-timer. (The fact that Rudy's trip was delayed also explains why Cornelia did not hear Mary Stahl's message. Because Rudy never called Cornelia while he was gone to tell her of his changed plans, she ended her housesitting on the 12th, not the 13th.)

3) The testimony of two particular people would prove very helpful in bringing the guilty party to justice. Which two people?

The people who would prove helpful in bringing the guilty party to justice are Mrs. Wheelock, who could confirm that Daphne had visited Rudy's home the day before the murder, and the delivery person, who could confirm that the slip of paper (or package) had been left prior to Daphne's arrival. The combination of these two testimonies would have been important in establishing Daphne's guilt.

SOLUTION TO "WARM-BLOODED MURDER" (page 13)

1) Who killed Vince Fernald and why?

Clancy McTigue was the guilty party. Here's what happened:

Sometime during the night prior to the primary, McTigue broke into the town hall in order to rig one of the voting machines in favor of his candidate, Michael Doucette. (Note that "Doucette" is next to "Dole" alphabetically. What McTigue did was to insert a paper strip that reversed the two candidates' names, confident that no one would notice the reversal.) Fernald, ready for bed and dressed in pajamas (in case you were wondering about the "scantily clad" part), looked outside from his nearby home and saw that something was amiss. He threw on his overcoat and went to check things out. That's when he came across McTigue, who killed him in the heat of the moment. McTigue then deposited the overcoat miles away in an unsuccessful attempt to get investigators looking in the wrong place.

2) How could the other suspects be ruled out?

The important point is that the murder occurred sometime very early Tuesday morning or even Monday night, as opposed to during the day on Tuesday, when McTigue had an alibi. How do we know this? Well, Clem Woolsey would ordinarily have removed the trash during the day on Tuesday, but his schedule had been altered because of the Presidents' Day holiday on Monday. Had his schedule been normal, it would have proved that the murder occurred after the trash pickup, but this was not the case. When Woolsey went to the town hall dumpster, he was simply checking out the trash to find out what was in store for him the following day! (The shift of one day also explains why he was seen in an area that appeared to be in violation of his schedule.)

Clem is of course a very unlikely suspect, because if he had shoved Fernald into the dumpster, he surely would have been silent about it, preferring to dump the body off the next morning. He might even have made a special trip to the town hall, the Monday holiday notwithstanding. Either way, he certainly wouldn't have called attention to his own misdeed!

As for Luc Evans-Wood, note that his remarks about the temperature seemed to support McTigue's innocence, because had it actually been five degrees Fahrenheit outside, the pool of blood would almost certainly have frozen had the body been there for any length of time. However, Evans-Wood is

Canadian and therefore would use the Celsius scale! Five degrees Celsius is 41 degrees Fahrenheit, well above the freezing level. We know that Evans-Wood is Canadian because he drove "down" to Jasper Falls—which, although fictitious, is located near Dixville Notch, in northernmost New Hampshire. Also, Evans-Wood received mail the previous day, which he couldn't have done had he been in the United States, because the U.S. Postal Service is closed on Presidents' Day. Most important of all, the fact that he is Canadian substantiates his claim that he had no particular interest in the outcome of the election. He certainly had no motive to be involved in either vote-tampering or the murder of Vince Fernald. (How's that for some heavy-duty sleuthing?)

And because Hugh Livingston had been out of town until driving back to post his vote that morning, he has an alibi for the only time that matters. All of which leaves Clancy McTigue. Although McTigue has an alibi throughout the day on Tuesday, the murder had already been committed.

3) How did an examination of the voting records help the investigation?

Although the voting records didn't indicate who voted for whom (the whole purpose of voting machines is to guarantee this privacy), they nonetheless contained some valuable information. First of all, although Vince Fernald was a deeply involved political operative who lived next door to the polling place, an examination of the records would have revealed that he never even voted that day! Had he been alive, he would surely have voted promptly in the morning, but this time around he couldn't, for obvious reasons. This was yet more powerful evidence that the murder had occurred prior to the polls being open.

In addition, the voting records would have confirmed Clancy McTigue's story—that he hadn't voted until the middle of the afternoon. (Although individual votes aren't recorded, voters' names would be systematically checked off as they reached the polling place.) The reason McTigue waited until the afternoon to vote was that he could go into the rigged booth and remove the phony paper strip after a meaningful bloc of votes had accumulated. That's why the machine looked normal to the investigators—and that completes the case!

SOLUTION TO "WHERE THERE'S A WILL" (page 61)

1) Who killed Marion Webster?
The killer was Gwen.

2) Where was the murder weapon hidden after the crime?
Before the murder, Gwen had hollowed out one of the thick reference books in her father's study. That's where she placed the murder weapon immediately following the killing. It didn't occur to the bungling first team of investigators to look within the study itself. (You did better, I'm sure. It's an old trick.) At some point she had a chance to go in and replace the hollow book with a real one.

3) Which of the children was Webster going to treat harshly in his revised will? (One of them is the killer!)
Marion Webster had decided to change his will to give Gwen a fake necklace ("put on ice") instead of the family heirloom. That was her motive. The others to be treated harshly by their father were Herbert (who had a fine "past as a lad," but who had disappointed his father thereafter) and Dorothy (whose library donations were going to be reduced.)
Note that of the three losers in Webster's to-be-revised will, only Gwen's whereabouts were not accounted for. She alone had motive and opportunity.
The "winners" included Eugene (Gene), as tipped off by Webster saying that "Gene rates income"—meaning that he should receive the bond portfolio. The other two winners were Biff and Laura, who benefited from their father saying

that "funding for 'libraries' would increase." Laura (late September) was a Libra and Biff (April 1) was an Aries. The "signs getting crossed" was a reference to the fact that the word "libraries" forces the two signs of the zodiac to share the letter "a." And that's a wrap!

Index